# COSSACK IDEALIST

I0735598

## MJ Politis, Ph.D.

276 5th Avenue Suite 704 #944

New York, NY 10001

Copyright © 2024 M. J. Politis

ISBN (Paperback) 978-1-918130-79-9

ISBN (Hardback) 978-1-918130-80-5

ISBN (eBook) 978-1-918130-78-2


All rights reserved

This novel is entirely a work of fiction. The names, characters and incidents portrayed in it are the work of the author's own imagination. Any resemblance to actual persons, living or dead, locations or events is purely coincidental.

No part of this publication may be reproduced, stored in a retrieval system, copied in any form or by any means, electronic, mechanical, photocopying, recording or otherwise transmitted without written permission from the publisher. You must not circulate this book in any format.


Cover Design by Woodbridge Publishers.

Find out more about our upcoming releases and authors at www.woodbridgepublishers.com and sign up for our newsletter to stay updated!

Dedicated to you…the reader. With appreciation for your
being open to this offering.

And all those I have known who made this offering
possible.

# CHAPTER 1

So, why should you read the story I want, and need, to tell you about Stefan Denosevich, a lovable, kind and idealistic Ukrainian Cossack private who was transformed into something else by his own hand, and mine, in World War I and in many other forgotten wars that happened soon after it was over? Because you want to know about what really happened to the Cossacks who allowed Mother Russia to become a world power under the Czars, and then the Red Commissars later? Because the Cossacks, named such after the Turkish word 'kazak' meaning 'free man', represent the boldest, most noble and expressive nature of the Slavic people when sober and on occasion when drunk? Or because you wish YOU could get on a horse and gallop across the Steppes liberating hard-working and oppressed people while singing and dancing in the saddle? Or you heard stories about how they lived by their own rules, democratically, and in the service of God, in their own villages in their heyday? Or you're interested in what happened to Stefan Denosevich when he underwent his own experiment with different moralities during an immoral time as an idealist who always saw the best in people and animals, in the worst of times?

But, first, let me introduce myself, partially anyway, as it connects to the story. A tale which, in YOUR century and continent, has more relevancy than you think, or can easily imagine. As for who I was to Stefan, well, various descriptors can be said. They are, in some way, all true and accurate. I was, and perhaps still am, his teacher and student. His master and servant. Some would say an elderly ancestor born of the once Cossack-run Steppes and a freak of nature whose origins were never known to Ukrainians, Russians, or anyone else in his time. Some would speculate that I was a magician who was, and maybe still is, a master healer, torturer, and (some say anyway) savior. More about me later.

But first, when you read the word 'Cossack,' the image that first comes to mind is a man and his horse, the latter willing to do anything for that man, including galloping into cannon fire. But only at the request of the right Cossack who plunked his ass on top of the saddle. The 37 years still young between the ears. Stefan knew so little about people, but he knew horses.

The main character in our story, set in the first quarter of the twentieth century, was more accurately a small-framed but adequately muscular boy in a man's body who could still not grow more than a thin mustache on his angelic face. It was topped off with a cropped head between his elephant ears, which featured a non-regulation Ukrainian Cossack warlock that he hid under his tall fur hat when the Imperial Russian inspectors came to inspect the 'Little Russians'. He was an 18th-century horseman daydreamer born into the late, rapidly mechanizing 19th century who had Cossack roots and inclinations to be as free as his ancestors had been. His blue eyes complemented his smiling face. His compulsion to serve exhausted him as he didn't know the difference between serving and pleasing. The 30-something 'lad' considered it an honor to serve the Lord while being underserved, and abused, by his fellow soldiers, childhood friends, wife, and children.

It is appropriate to begin his story in 1916, while he was serving (and trying to overplease) his fellow Conscripts and 'his Excellency' the Czar, in a Ukrainian Cossack Cavalry unit commanded, of course, by Russian officers.

In his capacity of conscripting unwilling stray or captured horses to join the Imperial Army at the Front, Stefan tried to 'reach an agreement with' rather than 'beat into submission' the steeds. In a war more deadly to four-legged equines than two-legged humans. Which specific technique would work best to train the newest equine arrival to the coral was up for grabs at the transit Camp, half a day's ride on horse, a full day's march by foot, and a one-hour truck ride from the Austrian lines on a muddy and cold March in 1916. "An Arab head, with Thourobred legs and Quarterhorse feet, who is trying to figure out who he is and where he came from like the rest of us… who is in conflict with himself, no doubt, " Stefan commented to his fellow conscripts regarding the latest horse captured from the Austrians in the last '(as the newspaper reporters wrote anyway) 'light skirmish',' Where a quarter of the men on both sides were given the opportunity to see first hand if the heaven the priests said admitted bold soldiers fighting for their country with open arms really did exist. The most virtuous of the dead would be reunited with previously departed relatives who made it past the Pearly Gates for a forever joyous Christmas dinner that lasted all year long. Or if the recently dead soldiers had been born into abusive families or had nagging wives, they would be spared that dreaded fate.

But for the moment, Stefan's attention was on the horse with enlarged eyes and a massive space between them where the gelding could do a lot of thinking and feeling. "He has a head that thinks for himself, and eyes that have taken in a lot," the master horse trainer and self-taught practitioner of veterinary as well as human medicine commented as he gently stroked the mostly healed wounds on the side of the Austrian steed's neck. He blew into the steed's nostrils, singing between breaths a German nursery song which was always a sure-fire way to begin a dialogue in verbal commands, or rather 'requests'. Only to have his hairless chin wacked by the horse's snout, with open teeth that he avoided by quickly pulling back. Stefan's subsequent fall was broken by a pile of straw on which there was a generous layer of excrement from the last horses he had brought back into service by ministering to their wounds and their frightened minds.

"So, this one can detect my Ukrainian accent," Stefan said by way of explanation as a chorus of laughs came in from his fellow conscripts safely OUTside the round pen.

Wiping what he could from his now brown ass, Stefan leaped back on his feet. He grabbed hold of the rope connected to the horse's bridle. After some tugs and releases, the horse finally stopped trying to take Stefan for a ride through the muck. The proud cut gelding's ears went forward, his front foot lashed at the overgrown Cossack lad, nailing him in his left calf.

"He's a mean one," Sergeant Petro Boyko grumbled from the safe side of the hastily built round pen, though his oversized cheeks were covered with a straggly beard, the air emanating from his somehow always over-fed mouth stinking of an extra ration of breakfast vodka. "That proud cut gelding is more valuable to us as a stud than as a saddle or draft horse." He pulled his rifle away from his gigantic over-haired shoulders, aiming its barrel at the thus far, and for good reason, uncooperative horse's head.

"No!" Stefan yelled out, putting himself between the horse, who was trying to kick some sense into him, and the trigger-happy Sergeant's bullet. "This horse is shell-shocked, or trained to hate people who look like us, talk like us, or smell like us," Stefan proposed with the utmost sense of urgency. "I know that we're in more need of food than the officers are in need of horses, but…" he pleaded with the supply Sergeant who doubled as a cook. Who was rumored to put human flesh into his 'Austrian stew', which he sold on the black market for money he put in his own pocket. Of course, such was only a rumor, to Stefan anyway. "Please, let me show you how useful this horse could be to all of us alive," Stefan pleaded. "If treated with kindness, any mean man or beast will become kind, good, and useful in good ways, right?"

The Ukrainian Sergeant left the decision regarding that to the men under him. Like the horse, "So, what do you say regarding the medicine boy's claim regarding human and animal nature? Should we give him the chance to test his theory? A show of hands!"

Ten of the twelve human rights arms present went up. Some had been injured by Austrian bullets and others by fist fights with their fellow soldiers during the long periods of boredom between 'noble battles'. All of them had been stitched up or otherwise mended by Stefan. A conscript whose flesh was, somehow, never pierced by any bullet, bayonet, or shrapnel in any skirmish. Begrudgingly, the supply Sergeant lowered his rifle. "Proceed with the experiment, then, Private Denosevich," he instructed Stefan. "But if this horse sends you to the Lord in Heaven---"

"---It's because it is God's Will, and you can feed my body to whatever creature needs it," Stefan said, taking off his Imperial Russian Army coat, tunic, then his hat, shaking his Cossack warlock at the horse. Bare-chested against an early winter wind, he pulled out a carrot from under his sash, offering it to the new equine 'prisoner of war.' It was accepted, but with caution.

"Better to scare or punish that wildie with a shashka," Ukrainian-born and bred Corporal Olek Koval said, pulling out his sword. It was a single-blade weapon his grandfather obtained from a Tatar freedom fighter in the Caucasus when in the service of the Imperial Army sent by the Czar to liberate the Georgian Islamic 'pagans' so they could be saved by the Russian Orthodox Jesus. "A weapon you only use when charging 'imaginary enemies', 'Doctor' Stefan!" the thin-faced, naturally balding, overly mustached thirty-year-old 'can fix anything you can break, but you owe me a big favor' mechanic continued. "A sword which---"

"---Is still strapped to my side, and which I use to scare the enemy so they run away, or surrender, for their own good so we can advance our noble causes to liberate the oppressed," Stefan shot back. "Like my noble ancestors, Stenka Razin, Kandraty Rulavin, Bohdan Khemennytsdy and-"

"---Maybe Yemelyan Pugachev, still PRIVATE Stefan Denosivich?" Imperial Captain Nicholi Ivanov shouted as he strode to the coral, his back arched like a White Russian officer from Moscow, in keeping with his aristocratic roots. "A pretender who claimed he was an incarnation of Peter the Second, murdered by his wife, Czarina Catherine the Great?"

"And who inspired Cossacks, serfs, peasants, Old Believer priests, and enlightened Slavs AND Tatars to rise up against Catherine's oppressive reign!" Stefan proclaimed proudly.

"And lost, at the cost of his followers' lopped-off daydreaming heads," Ivanov reminded the lad. "Yes, Pugachev, a Cossack who was considered a thief, scoundrel, and mentally deranged lunatic by many of his own people. Who was as deluded as you are about your bloodlines and what the noble grandfathers of yours really did. The factual books say that your Ukrainian and Russian Cossack ancestors actually---"..

"----Did what they had to do under the circumstances, Your Honor, Sir," Stefan shot back while edging a blanket towards the horse, laying it gently on its back. Hiding, or perhaps not believing, the fact that many of his noble ancestors were no strangers to massacring countless numbers of Indigenous pagans while 'civilizing' Yakuts in Siberia and Muslims in the Caucasus if they resisted Russian Orthodox Christianity or paying taxes to the Czar. And putting aside the fact that Cossacks were assigned the special duties of burning live bodies and still populated buildings in Jewish villages. "The books in Moscow are WRONG!" Stefan squeaked out, hoping it was perceived as a bark. "We were fighting for our freedom. And the right to rule our own land in the Steppes!" Stefan continued as he eased a blanket and then a saddle onto the steed trained by his Austrian masters to attack Russian soldiers, and conditioned by gunfire to not trust ANYone in uniform. "We Cossacks fought for special favors and freedoms the Czar gave us, yes. But mostly for the honor of serving Christ, Mother Russia, and humanity."

"For which you Cossacks were, and are now, well paid in MONEY!" the White Russian Captain from Moscow added. "And once the money stops, all of you Cossacks will desert and get a better deal from the other side," the anti-Cossack and even more so anti-Ukrainian officer continued, raising up his clean-shaven chin, looking downward at the enlisted Ukrainian 'Little Russians.'

"No, we won't! desert!" Stefan insisted, after which he sang a Cossack love song to the horse, in Ukrainian in notes that were more off than on key. "Cossacks fight for honor. Not money," he then proclaimed after having inflicted auditory pain on the horse and humans within range of his voice. "Yes, the Czar is giving special favors to our families back home in Ukraine. Which will very soon be an independent country again. Run by democratic rule in the service of its own people. And in the service of the Russian Czar. Who will bless our independence as Slavs in the service of one God, one world, and one common vision for humanity, where each gives according to his or her abilities, and takes according to his or her needs."

"Of course, you men will not desert," the Aristocratic-born and conditioned Russian Captain said with a smirk at the Socialist pipe dream which was adopted by an unanticipated number of women as well as penis-bearing 'commoners.' He looked behind him to the Ukrainian Cossack conscripts, laying his hand on the handle of his revolver. "Right?"

"Yes, sir. Yes, Your Honor," the unarmed enlisted men answered with bowed heads and forced smiles to the Russian Captain who was known to be the fastest draw in the East AND West. And who had the reputation of being able to put a bullet into the head of any man who even thought differently than he did before that thought could be converted to voice. Captain Ivanov had put bullets into the backs of more than a handful of recruits who knew that it was a smarter military decision to survive a losing battle by retreating rather than continuing a futile attack. "But for the moment, let's all enjoy a joke together," the Imperial Army officer continued. "Including the 'good doctor' who sees the good in everything and everyone who---"

"---Is about to get on this horse and prove to you that even in a demon horse there is an angel who is stronger, Sir, who---" Stefan said, pushing his belly onto, then his ass into the saddle. The horse took three strong strides at a walk, then eased into a collected trot. Just as 'an agreement' was in the works, Stefan heard something click under the horse's feet. "A snake!' he whispered to the frightened horse regarding the legless creature which had been thrown into the pen by one of the conscripts, or (according to Stefan, anyway) the whims and Will of the Deity Who created them. "It's a snake that won't hurt you," he assured the steed, after which the Austrian gelding reared up, throwing Stefan on the muddy ground, his head landing in a wad of frozen manure.

A thunderous, liberating laughter blasted into the air, shared equally by all ranks. While handing over money from wagers made regarding the outcome of the angelic doc vs the demonic beast 'showdown', the Cossack recruits and the Russian Captain made jokes, as equals. Each dig at Stefan was wittier than the last. They included "Shit for brains meets more shit". "A new method to turn dumb angels into smart devils". "Sometimes brains need to be shaken up, like borsht". "A sure-fire way to shake some brains into an empty-headed daydreamer". And, from the Captain, "So, you see, our court jester does know how to brighten up our day."

As Stefan regained full consciousness, he recalled something from his childhood.as the butt of everyone else's jokes in the village he grew up in where he was always injuring or embarrassing himself somehow. It was an instinct and an assigned job granted to him as a Blessing by God. Such made everyone laugh, providing badly needed humor for everyone. Yes, here he was to be a 'morale officer' in the same way. However, the insignia of that rank was something only he could see. And the horse that threw him off might see as well as long as the rebellious Austrian steed negotiated his relationship with his Slavic captors and feeders carefully.

"Yeah, I know," Stefan said, his ass still on the ground, when looking into the eyes of the steed as the horse stood still, staring down at him as if to say, 'ok, we both aren't where we want to be, so do you have any solutions for this?'.

Stefan smiled at the beast, addressing him with direct eye contact, "You, my friend, are like Hershal Kominski, the Jewish tailor and comic who kept us Christian soldiers entertained back where I grew up…The schlamele, which is you, spills the soup on the schlimazel, which is me." He took in a deep breath under his hurting and possibly broken ribs as he edged his way onto his aching feet. "And as for that snake the captain put under your feet, well, that's just a prop the audience put onto the stage. In the service of all of us, including YOU," he continued, looking up at the Heavenly Father.

"You can use a good laugh too," he said, wiping his aching and even more odorous ass. Enjoying the pain, somehow.

# CHAPTER 2

You may be asking, how was I able to see, hear, and smell what was going on around Stefan as well as what was going on between his 'selective hearing' ears and behind his 'seeing but not seeing' eyes? Well, I had many spies in his vicinity when I was not able to be physically present, particularly after he joined up to fight for a democracy-promoting Czar against the evil German Kaiser and partner in slime, the Emperor of the Austro-Hungarian Empire. But who was I really working for? And why? Well, maybe you can figure it out as you keep reading. And if you find out, please tell me. But let us save such mysteries for a later time.

For the moment, suffice it to say that I was the most needed and therefore unnoticed member of Stefan's small company of Cossacks that had been decimated into an oversized platoon due to 'heroic actions' they had undertaken during the first two years of this war to end all wars.

After Stefan reached an agreement involving the horse, which was favorable to both parties, his unit was ordered to move West towards the Front lines and encountered en route refugees going in the other direction. These displaced civilians were carried by horseback, their own tired feet, or each other. Those unable to stand were cargo in wagons pulled by both men and beasts.

Stefan thought about the men he was serving in his capacity as a medic, horse doctor, scout, and butt of jokes which needed to be amplified to keep up the spirits of his comrades. While mounted on the proud cut Austrian gelding, he looked at the men he was serving with, struggling with squinted eyes and a pounding head to figure out why they became who they seemed to be, to him anyway.

"Yes, Seargent Boyko is giving meat to Elena, the young gypsy widow refugee who is now responsible for three children, one that looks like her and one who looks very much like him, by sheer coincidence of course," Stefan said to the Austrian equine 'mutt' between his legs, in broken Ukrainian and as well as much accentless German he could muster. "And the bread he is requesting in return is most probably loaded with more mold than barley or wheat. Saving her children from a stomach ache and her children from seeing nightmares while they are still awake. Is that not so, Achilles?"

"As Stefan perceived it, the horse snorted in approval to his new name, and Stefan's attempt to convert the wild Austrian beast into a bilingual steed. The horse took note of the generosity of Boyko to Elena and the mixed family he had presumably never met, and would never see again.

Meanwhile, Stefan went on to relate stories to Achilles', or more accurately, ME, MY in Ukrainian, which translated into English were….

As for Corporal Kiral, the fees he was requesting, and getting, for fixing a truck filled with wounded civilians stuck on the side of the road were no doubt for supplies he would buy in the next village. To be returned by him as soon as he could race back to them with equipment to fix the truck, and medical supplies to repair the broken human flesh inside of it. And besides, Kiral had lost his hair way too early. Of course, he deserved payment in the form of a two-foot lock of hair from a moderately wounded and penniless mother who voluntarily cut it off, giving it to him as pre-payment for coming back to cure her badly wounded child.

Regarding Captain Nicholi Ivanov, yes he was an arrogant Russian Officer from Moscow, but his riding in front of the column on the tamest and whitest horse in the company was needed for morale. And since he was the brains of the outfit, it was appropriate for him to have gotten triple rations of breakfast a few hours earlier. After all, a full belly is required for a healthy mind.

There were others in the company, which was now reduced to being a platoon and a half. Vlodymir Melnyk was entitled to wear the heaviest and oversized coat available since he was a thin man under it. And of course, the medals overloading his chest were well earned, despite the fact that when he was drunk, the stories about how he got each of them kept changing. They couldn't have been stolen from dead or wounded comrades in battle, or those who had lost them in a card game.

And that good luck necklace of ears around Dimitri Sokolov's neck had to be from pigs rather than Austrians slain in battle, or fellow Slavs who he had knocked senseless in the taverns he had liberated from the enemy.

At a rest stop, Stefan looked at the hopeful external presentation of the 'camp' that had been set up by the meeting of soldiers going to the Front and civilians retreating from it. I, of course, was cursed, or blessed, with seeing the worms and putrid fruit underneath that bright red apple offered to me. Breaking the reflective silence, or deadly quiet, was a rendition of a folk song I recalled from my own childhood played on a refugee's violin, Olek's mandolin, and then the most ancient and expressive musical instrument, a young girl's human voice. Stefan smiled, as did, eventually, in one way or the other, the men serving with him. They felt every bit of the music as if it were a gourmet-cooked stew laden with medicinals sent by the Almighty to nurture body, mind, and soul. To me, that song, which emanates through and converts the blood and smoke-tinted ethers into a clear blue spring sky, was just…notes. Sounds are emitted into the air. That, by sheer chance, changed their pitch and volume as the wind changed direction.

I looked at the distant hills to the right and the left, noting the leaf-bearing trees that had not yet been turned into charred sticks. My ears detected birds within those trees, adding something that could double as harmony to the song created by two-legged musicians in the all-too-temporary rest camp. To which a few of the soldiers and the still ambulating refugees danced. I felt the earth under my feet undergo a certain vibration, feeling a wave of unexpected approval meandering up my spine . If allowed to let my perception of the present drift into the past, it felt like a hopeful future was upon all of us. Until the birds stopped singing, and then those in the forest to the right fled with alacrity eastward towards the Motherland we were, theoretically, protecting. It was followed by the avian chorus from the left forest taking to winged flight towards the same destination. Every horse with half a brain still left in its skull pointed their ears towards the Front. Such was followed by thunder, first from the sky in that direction, then from human sources.

"Big guns from the Austrians this time," I heard from Sergeant Boyko as the clear blue sky at the Front was penetrated by clouds of black soot. "Forty millimeter shells," he said, sniffing the air with his oversized nostrils. "Which smells like--"

"---Victory for us after we overrun them! Sneaking our way towards them, undetected under the fog rolling into what is left of the forest, to their weakest point. Then and only then, we attack them!" Captain Ivanov asserted. Half of the men under his command began to slither away and join the refugees as they began their retreat Eastward towards fellow still-home-owning Slavs or strangers who perhaps would welcome them, or perhaps would not. "And if anyone has any other thoughts that are different," Ivanov said as he quickly pulled out his revolver. He fired a round at the feet of Corporal Olek just before the latter was about to put a bullet into his Commander's back.

From what I could surmise from the grumblings amongst the enlisted men, Olek's desire to send his Commander to his just or unjust reward in retribution for said commander having shot three of Olek's former comrades for retreating from a losing battle before the official command for 'pull back' was given. "We WILL be victorious against the Austrians," Ivanov said to the soldiers still under his command on this not-so-fine day. "Because…." he blasted out, his non-shooting hand up in the air. He flickered his fingers so as to signal his men to bellow out a thunderous battle cry that would scare the Austrians back to Vienna. "Because!" he repeated, having gotten no reply from his men, who were contemplating how to initiate the long-needed mutiny and the consequences of following through with it. "Because!!?" Ivanov repeated again and again, pointing his revolver at the men with the angry and vengeful blue eyes. His stare shifted from one potential leader of the mutiny to the next. The message spread like a wave through each of them, discouraging even the thought of mutiny in all of them.

All of the potential mutineers remained silent, their thoughts and plans of liberating themselves buried under fear. Until Stefan, whose kind face remained hopeful and obedient, spoke up, questioning the Captain's message. "We will be victorious, because we are in this together?" he both proposed and asked. "And because we are fighting for a just cause?" the child in the man's body asserted, framing the statement as a question. "And because right will be converted into might, with the help of the Almighty?" he went on, after which he gazed up and into the sky. "Right?" he asked the God whom he never lost faith in.

Another moment of collective reflection swarmed over the men. Each of them looked at each other and into themselves, somehow both at the same time. It was as if Stefan had really connected to the Deity above the shrapnel-filled clouds and inside all of the living and the dead below them. Stefan finally lowered his head, providing the men with an answer. "Yes!" he declared, hugging each man in what was left of the Company. "God, who created the fog up ahead, IS with us. I know it. And we all should know it as we work to save each other. And to win this next battle, destroying more of the Austrians' weapons and sparing the men who operate them. Sending as many Austrians home in retreat, or taking ALL of them as prisoners this time, so we all can be brothers after this war is over!"

"In a world where…"

"…There are no Aristocratic Ivanovs in Russia or Austria," I heard from Olek, the peasant enlisted man staring at and into the Imperial Army Captain's face.

"And the Czars are in service of the people rather than the other way around?" the once anti-Socialist Melnik offered.

"And we compete for national superiority with cooking contests rather than wars, where we kill each other and put the meat we gather up into our own stew?" Sergeant Boyco speculated.

"And these medals we get are for saving men, women, and children rather than killing or re-locating them?" Melnick asked as he jiggled the medals on his chest, some of which he actually did earn rather than steal.

"And I can go home to my wife and mistresses, who I love in different ways, with none of them finding out about the other?" Sokolov let flow through a warm smile, rather than a sadistic grin of delight which came to his face whenever lopping off an ear, finger, or nose from a dead or dying enemy combatant. Or rivalry over a bar wench, a fellow Cossack fell in love with after ingesting too much vodka.

"Yes, and I can go back to studying philosophy and music at Saint Petersburg, rather than War and Politics at the University of Moscow," Captain Ivanov related, after which he voiced a very on-key rendition of an aria from 'Boris Gudinov.'

"Yes!" Stafan said, exclaimed, then proclaimed to the sky, which cleared up, miraculously. And then turned silent. Followed by mocking laughter from the men around him.

"Fool!" "Idiot," "A daydreamer," "Wishful thinker who can't think at all". Echoed through Stefan's elephant ears.

"Except when he's taking bullets out of you, stitching up your wounds, or somehow keeping the horses you overuse in ridable rather than eatable shape!" I said to the laughing men regarding the one who was not laughing at all, which fell on deaf ears, once again.

Just as there is an inequality of wealth in the world that will always be around, no matter what compassionate theology or democratic form of government exists, the gap between the respected and non-respected widened that moment until it was interrupted by a cloud of dust approaching from the West. Followed by a rumbling of the earth under all of our feet. Followed then by an army of Austrians who only saw in front of them Russian Soldiers who had to be eliminated. In the service, of course, of Selective Compassion. Caring for one's family and countrymen first, second, and last, leaving no consideration for the welfare of a stranger or foreigner. Justifying starving 'others' of bread and water so that 'your own' could dine with filet mignon and champagne. After all, the death of a Russian Soldier, who has a family back home in Moscow or Kiev, secures the safety and well-being of an Austrian family in Vienna.

# CHAPTER 3

It is said that in the heat of battle, combatants become who they never were. Or perhaps they become who they always have been, as survival is what is at stake, not social status or likability, unless you are a Russian aristocratic Captain leading Ukrainian recruits from behind. And would soon be pulled into making decisions that would affect everybody, and even more notably, himself.

The trenches where Stefan, his comrades, and their horses took shelter, presumably without the Austrians knowing they had arrived, were deep enough to protect them from the machine gun fire thanks to the Hungarian Peasants working as labor battalions for the Austrian High Command two months earlier. When they were overrun by the Russian Army, the sandbag wall had been increased by two feet in height, complemented by dugouts resembling caves which primitive men and women had dug into the ground 10,000 years ago. Topped off with remnants of a roof added by political prisoners with the last of the trees, which had been the thickest forest in Western Ukraine. As usual, there were more equine bones embedded in the muck than human ones, the rats being the only well-fed still-breathing life forms. Something most of the military photographers from Vienna or Moscow didn't take pictures of, of course.

"So," Stefan said when glancing at a petrified wooden slab surface which had imprinted on it 'fuck the Czar', 'damn the Kaiser' and 'for a good time call...' with names of a number of women, and men, in the back lines. "It's good to be home again," he said, recalling his last two shifts in that same trench... "Even if we're allowed to be here for only half of this War to end all Wars."

"A line that President Wilson will be using to get the Americans' doughboys into the War," Corporal Kiral grunted as he scratched out the name of the pleasure woman in Kiev on the slab, the rocks, edging in another woman's name that Stefan didn't recognize. "Yes, the Doughboys who Wilson promised would come here, very soon."

"Named Doughboys because they make great white bread that beats our brown bread?" Stefan inquired, feeling the rumbling of his empty belly, his nostrils imagining the aroma of freshly-baked rolls.

"Because the American doughboys collect the dough, meaning money, from selling weapons, oil, and equipment to us, and them, Stefan," the childless Captain Ivanov noted while pointing to the Austrians huddled behind a well-built trench 2 hundred yards to the West. Addressing the most entertaining Cossack and useful medic under his command by his first name, a form of address he never gave to anyone else. This time his paternal instinct had a kind, bordering on envying expression, rather than being ashamed of and angered at Stefan's ignorance of the world as it is, and the hardcore belief Stefan had in how it should be. Again, Ivanov reflected on how the militarily inept private, whose bullets never hit their target, had acquired medical skills in taking out bullets from mutilated flesh that outclassed any medical officer in the Army. Still, Ivanov couldn't determine why neither Stefan nor he had ever been wounded, with regard to flesh anyway.

Ivanov took a deep breath into his pushed-out chest, adjusting his mind to the situation at hand. He wondered how, this time, he could keep Private Denosevic out of harm's way. Then, abruptly, he turned into a raging animal after he noted the name of the 'wonderful wench' named in the advertisement written in Russian Cyrillic as well as Austrian German. "Who put my beloved's first name and maiden name on this 'advertisement' for the 'best whore in Moscow?!" he demanded as he stared at Corporal Sokolov while the latter continued to busy himself collecting teeth, ears and scalps of dead Austrians.

After getting an 'how the hell should I, a commoner Cossack, know, your Excellency?' shrug as an answer, Ivanov pushed the inquiry to Sergeant Boyko. Ivanov grabbed him by his tunic and beard, pulling out a fistful of lice-infested mud-soaked hair.

"God knows, and, since He is not answering any of our questions about why we are here, I suppose we will never know, Sir," Boyko replied with a humble bow.

"But maybe YOU do?" Ivanov yelled into Corporal Kiral's face.

Putting on the poker face that won him extra rations of food, drink, and a warm blanket on cold moonlit nights made bearable by card playing, Kiral pointed to the Austrians on the other side of the charred, sulfurous rat-infested no-man's land in front of the trench through holes in the thick fog.

"And they will pay for defaming my beloved!" Ivanov pushed through gritted teeth, whipping out his sword with his slashing right fist, and his revolver with his left. "We are going over the top, lads! Now!" he yelled to the men, this time with the intent of leading the charge. "And all of you are DEAD!" he grunted to the Austrians in his best German. "You perverts, demented demons, and bastards will pay for violating Elena Putinov's honor!"

"We're right behind you, Sir!" Corporal Kolov assured his superior, placing his assuring bear-like hand on his Captain's shaking shoulder. After which he slowly shifted his gaze to fellow conscripts Sokolov, Boyco, and Melnik.

"I will lead the charge this time! To demand satisfaction!" Ivanov ordered and pledged. "We have the element of surprise, since I am certain that they can't see us, but we can see them, because they have not fired at us yet."

"As you wish, Sir," Boyco replied, snapping a filled magazine of bullets of his rifle.

"For Mother Russia!" Melnik, a Ukrainian Nationalist who hated the Czar more than dysentery, rats, and trenchfoot, yelled out, adjusting the bayonet on his rifle. "And Elena!" he added.

All of the enlisted Cossacks, with the exception of Stefan, shared all-knowing smiles and winks of the eye behind their commanding officer's back. All the while, blind rage took over Ivanov's ocular portholes and the overeducated brain behind them. It was enhanced fivefold when he looked at the locket hanging around his neck.

Any fool could see that putting the Aristocratic and somehow never even wounded Captain's beloved's name (that he muttered with affection in his sleep while sporting a wide smile and ejaculation of sperm from his crotch) on the posterboard was a shared endeavored led by Boyco, Melnick, and Koval. Designed to get their 'beloved commander' to lead the next deadly charge instead of orchestrating it from behind, because of his 'genius as a military strategist,' of course. Was Elena Ivanov's wife, mistress, daughter or the always well groomed Captain's transvestite male's lover? And whose idea was it to be sure that Ivanov saw that name on the slab of wood? Such didn't seem to matter. At least to the Cossack who decided to take matters into his own hands."

"I will lead the charge this time!" Stefan exclaimed, grabbing a submachine gun buried in the mud under the front half of a dead Austrian soldier. He slung it around his shoulders with one hand, while pulling out his sainted and always victorious Grandfather's sabre with the other. He hopped on me. "Are you prepared to do the honorable thing? God will protect us if we do! I promise you that!"

"Better use the machine gun rather than your sword," Boyco yelled out as Stefan inserted both of his feet into the stirrups.

"And take cover behind your soon-to-be dead horse!" Koval warned Stefan as his I started to buck, after a mortar blew a hole no less than 20 feet in front of him. Stefan requested me to move in a choppy gallop, breaking through the coral holding the other Russian horses, sending all of them in separate directions before they could be caught. Ivanov ordered the men to catch the horses, but neither he nor the Cossacks had any success at such.

"So," I thought as more mortars blew up around the trenches, causing no harm to man or beast. "Warning shots," I thought, having been through this situation many times before. "The Austrians are more interested in live horses and interrogatable prisoners than regained real estate," I said to myself. Stefan's machine gun dropped from his shoulders. He pulled out a sword, swinging it in the air in a motion that was both heroic and artistically breathtaking."

"Achilles, forward!" Stefan both asked and commanded. "God is with us!"

It is said that horses do not have a belief in any God, except compassion for those who have been kind to us, our herd, and the world. Why I let Stefan be the 'boss' and take me in charge of the Austrians, I, to this day, do not know.

But there was something about his conviction, the situation, and the need for me to go back to the Austrians who claimed to be my owners, who I actually owned. Stefan did a Cossack acrobatic dance on my back to avoid the onslaught of bullets, sometimes with his commands and sometimes on my own. I eased into equine ballet movements I learned while being trained to be an Austrian Lipizzaner to avoid mortars. It was a colorful way to commit suicide for both of us. But as the American cowboys in the Western novels and silent pictures said, 'ya gotta die of something.'

I had died before and been reincarnated into different forms. And as for being assigned to the body of a horse with mismatched breeding, placed into a war where the first casualties are both the innocence of men and the death of horses, maybe it was time to 'soul jump' into another life form? Hopefully, as a general with a humanoid body, he would have the common sense to surrender. Or an "Elena' who could, with her feminine charms, convince generals from both sides of this war to decide to do business together to obtain more colonies, wealth, and political positions rather than to build empires by depopulating and demolishing the countries that you want to acquire.

But, as it turned out, I and the naïve lad-man on my back wound up entertaining the Austrians with acrobatic leaps that nearly tore our legs out of their sockets as we both dodged directed mortar and small arms fire from BOTH sides of no man's land. Then, abruptly, the shooting and mini-bombardment stopped. The Austrian commanding officer yelled something to his men, raising up a white flag. The enlisted men on 'our' side of the trench halted firing.

I locked my legs in place, refusing to let Stefan do any other maneuvers with me. Boyco forced the business end of Ivanov's pistol down toward the so far bloodless dirt as he prepared to take down the Austrians who, so he imagined anyway, had had their way with Elena.

The Austrian commander, a Major by the looks of the intact half of his overcoat, applauded Stefan and me with the enthusiasm of an audience in prime balcony seats at his favorite opera. He then led his still-crouching men in a round of applause. Ivanov picked up a rifle, preparing to shoot the Austrian officer in the testicles, then the head, but was halted from doing so by Boyco, with a swift kick into his family jewels.

"A smart Sergeant you have there, Captain," the still-alive Austrian commander yelled out to Ivanov in grammatically correct, nearly accentless Russian. "As you can see, we are more than you are," continued, ordering his men to stand up and be counted... "But you're crazier than us, so we will let all go, you go back to the asylum you escaped from."

"Which weeee wwwwill!" Boyco slurred out of the left side of his mouth as an escaped inmate from a mental asylum, with jerky movements of his head. All the while putting his hand over Ivanov's mouth. imitating Stefan when his brain was flustered. "I ppprrommisse. Thhhannk Yyyouu fooor lllletting us gggooo home."

"Which we are defending, as is our God given right, honor, and duty!" Stefan proclaimed. "A place of justice, freedom, and beauty, and…"

Before Stefan could relate any more descriptors of a Motherland that gave no large portion of those three qualities to any of her 'children' except for the rich, powerful, or manipulative, I took HIM on another equine-human dance. I adjusted my hindlimbs with each buck so as to have him land back in the saddle rather than on his deluded head. Eventually, Stefan anticipated where I was taking him and enjoyed the ride.

"You know," the Austrian major said to Boyco while some of the men. "Your daydreaming circus performer on that crazy horse gave away your position. If not under strict control, he could be very dangerous, too, as you have heard."

"Himmmself and ootherrrss," Boyco replied in his best 'retarded' voice. "Lllikkeee the rest off usss, right?" he asked the platoon, which was now officially under his command, since Ivanov's mouth was still 'incapacitated' by Boyco's strong and now bitten bear-like hand.

His fellow conscripts agreed with 'yes's' pushed out of drooling and deformed lips.

"Hmmm," I heard the Austrian officer say to his second in command as I took the 'dance' towards him. "God protects fools and drunks. I pray to the God that I hope hasn't completely abandoned all of us that these fools didn't steal any vodka from the dead soldiers they got those guns and uniforms from."

With that, the Austrian officer received a message from a runner. After reading it, he motioned for his men to pack their belongings to move on to the next destination. As they filtered with their equipment to the North and South, I carried the more heart than brains 'rider' on my back towards 'home'. His home, anyway. With a well-designed buck, I threw Stefan onto the ground in a roll that landed his head on a pile of manure-caked mud rather than hard rock, rendering him in a more unconscious than conscious state, but still breathing.

While Stefan's fellow saner-than-they-ever-wanted-to-be fellow conscripts gathered around him, I gathered my equine brothers and sisters, returning them to their two-legged 'owners.' It took a lot to convince them to go back to the humans who romanticized about riding them to victory after they had been worn down by long rides, pulling heavy wagons, and being deprived of lush grasses to keep their tired muscles from atrophying. But most of their owners were Cossacks who, for the most part, did not consider a horse as a four-legged, non-petrol requiring transport machine or a source of portable food. Meanwhile, I watched from the corner of my eye and listened with my overly sensitive ears to what was occurring on what still was for the moment, 'our side of the line.

"Stefan almost got us all killed by giving away our position," Boyco reminded his subordinates. Ivanov helped my new 'master' to his feet, helping him drag his feet, then limp back to his Comrades, regaining more consciousness with each step.

Stefan was loaded up on a cart, which I, the least muscled in the herd, was assigned to pull. A choice I allowed to be made by reaching the wagon first. Melnik hopped into the driver's seat. "So, where to, Corporal Denosevic?" he asked Stefan.

"Sergeant Denosevic, you mean," Corporal Koval said with a congratulatory smile through his overgrown mustache.

'Lieutenant," Sergeant Boyco exclaimed, as he mounted his horse. "After he has a long, happy furlough at home, right, Captain?"

"A very long furlough indeed," Ivanov said as he looked into Stefan's confused eyes. "A very long furlough, my brave son, and comrade," he said, pulling two medals off Melnick's tunic. He pinned them securely to the bewildered lad-in-a-man's chest.

Melnick clenched his teeth in anger, with a forced smile. Particularly as one of those two medals was one that he had earned rather than stolen, one way or another. After the congregation had mounted up, or jumped into a wagon, they exited the trench just before a group of Austrian replacements moved into the already overmanned trench on the opposite side of no man's land. Then made their way on foot, slowly, to the back lines, doing their best to act like the mental patients they ridiculed and, truth be told, feared they might become one day.

"So, Achilles. One of these medals goes to you," now Sergeant soon to be Lieutenant Denosoic said in a loud voice. "We're both being promoted!"

"I snortled, agreeing with my 'master' who was too relieved and virtuous to believe the truth. That he was being sent back home so that he wouldn't endanger his Comrades anymore by charging an enemy who was too strong, numerous, armed, and smart to defeat. And for thinking with his heart rather than his head. Perhaps because of me or a soul a lot smarter than me manipulating and monitoring MY thoughts, he was able to, THIS time, turn a suicidal charge into a sacrificial dance. But the next 'song' in Stefan's opera would be experiencing an even more complicated libretto. His beloved family.

# CHAPTER 4

Stefan's next assignment was to go to Iankovia. A village hundreds of miles behind the Front where he was commanded, by royal decree and put into printed orders by Captain Ivanov, to see that the Iankovians who they are and do what they do. A village where Sergeant Stefan Denosovic's job was to facilitate 'profitable ventures for all concerned' on his way to becoming an officer. Maintaining the status quo till he was ready to be transferred to an even more important assignment. A village where, upon his arrival, Stefan noted that there were no other soldiers to command or be commanded by. A village which, according to the letter from High Command given to him after his delayed discharge from the field hospital, he had been elected 'mayor' in absentia by every one of its citizens. A village that was the 'pillar of stability, harmony and happiness', which was required to continue to be so to 'save Mother Russia from itself'. A village where Sergeant Stefan Denosivic was born, raised, and dreamt about coming back to as a decorated Slavic soldier and accomplished Cossack.

Indeed, by the way he leaned back on the saddle when riding into Iankovia as Sergeant Denosovic with a third medal given to him to join the two Ivanov had pinned to his chest, he made ME feel like I was the lead horse in a parade. And maybe I was. Even though the only followers of the future Lieutenant or Captain Mayor were mice, crows, and two stray dogs, they kept their distance. "Nicholi!" Stefan barked at a black and white mangy male hound trying to bite at my heels with each step I took. "Good to see you again, and that you have a girlfriend who respects as well as likes you," Stefan continued to the hound, throwing him pieces of beef jerky, noting a female dog behind him. "Best be careful about nipping at your new brother's heels," he said, pointing to my sweaty neck. "He doesn't mean to hurt you, but he might, by accident, of course. Because, Nicholi, I'm home for a while, finally."

Of course, I DID want to kick the aggressive and cowardly hound who was more interested in the jerky Stefan was throwing him than the 'man' who probably had raised him as a pup. Knowing my own strength and assessing the border collie-coyote cross's ignorance, I decided to merely postpone rather than cancel, giving the canine menace a lesson with my hoofs. But I suppose that Nicholi, who by the conversation Stefan still had with him, and the canine speak the dog was having with him, needed me to be 'Achilles' for a little while longer. At the same time, Sergeant Denosevic could continue to be Stefan for as long as he still could.

I let Stefan 'steer' me past houses built with old wood and slightly caved-in straw roofs housing animals, to one and two-story structures constructed with what looked and smelled like new lumber. With roofs covered with modern metal shingles rather than slabs of wood, smoke coming out of their brick chimneys. Telephone wires emerged from freshly planted poles, connecting each of the 31 houses occupied by two-legged mammals. The smells coming out of the partially opened kitchen windows, real ones made of glass, were from culinary delights far more exotic than borscht, porridge, and bread. Aromas that I recognized from the Austrian officers' club in the rear when I was in their service as a beast of burden for the enlisted men, and a sign of social status for their commanders. I never tasted French quiche, Belgian croissants, or Italian sausage, but I did vicariously enjoy seeing my 'masters' enjoy them and recall being given Swiss chocolate and apple strudel on more than one occasion. But that was another assignment. I hoped, and prayed, that this one would not wind up the same way.

"So, it looks like everyone here is doing far better than when I left, Achilles," Stefan commented while stroking my tense neck. "Proving that if you live honorably, give more than take, and serve the Deity within everyone, that Deity will give you back tenfold!" Stefan informed me as he continued prodding me onward, not stopping to let me have more than a mouthful of green grass, freshly harvested hay, or water. Against the audio backdrop of Stefan's empty stomach grumblings, accompanied by the acetone from his breath, my 'master' related the names and occupations of the beloved villagers. They all chose to stay in their houses, closing the blinds over their windows once we were spotted. A good, kind, and honest this and that,

Stefan said regarding the occupants of his family's 'welcoming' neighbors.

This 'common' village did have, according to Stefan anyway, a complete collection of commoner occupations. Baker, carpenter, blacksmith, woodsman, butcher, seamstress, and a new one, machine mechanic. All of which, of course, served the needs of the body and not the mind in a newly expanding town that included everything except a bookstore.

"And that is our church," Stefan proudly exclaimed as he, THANK GOD (who we horses seek to know and know about), brought me to a halt, allowing me to fill my belly with grass and water in front of the still-tallest building in the village. "And inside, Father Basili, writing a sermon, negotiating with God on our behalf," he continued, pointing to a window behind which the Good Father was seated at his desk, agonizing over a paper in front of his tired eyes. "And that's his secretary, Nadia Petrovitch, who helps him with the grammatical details and translations," he said as a woman with long, brown hair put her hands on Father Basili's shoulders, taking away the paper, then turning to him and edging her young face towards his. She then rubbed with her smiling chin his nearly all white beard, her hand moving downward between his legs as he laid down his pen and paper. He opened his mouth, the smile on it indicating that he was experiencing the kind of Bliss he would never describe in any sermon. Upon being spotted by us, Father Basili looked towards Stefan, or maybe to me. But before he could provide any comment, Nadia pulled down the window shade.

"Nadie speaks French and adds, as they say, 'spice to the sermon' that is tasteful and appropriate," Stefan said of the woman who I heard whisper words of love of body rather than Soul or Spirit to the Good Father. The Good Father exhaled moans of delight, mixed in with 'Yes, mistress, yes,' which Stefan, of course, didn't or wouldn't hear. "Father Basili and Nadia have very profound conversations about how to serve the Lord," he informed me.

Ironically, Stefan was a master of putting together flesh that disease or trauma had torn apart. But he knew so little about the anatomy between the legs. It's use for pleasure anyway. I thought about making a noise, to disrupt the 'theological discourse' between Basili and Nadia, but before I could say anything, Stefan pulled me onward to the last and most pothole-laden road in the village. "It's finally time to go home," Stefan informed me. "No, time for US to go home," he repeated, patting me on the neck, exuding a smile whose warmth and assurance were irresistible. And with a gentle prod of his boots on my flank, we proceeded forward at a trot,

The new Sergeant and soon-to-be Lieutenant Cossack sang 'The Cossack Rode over the Danube', the battle cry of the Cossacks when they went to war and the victory song they emitted with parched voices upon their return, no matter what the outcome of the battle.

When rounding each of the curves in the winding road, I envisioned our final destination, fields of wild grass. With even wilder horses grazing on them, kicking their heels up in the snow that defiantly lingered until the coming of summer. With old men sporting white warlocks teaching their grandsons how to shoot an arrow. At the same time, those grandsons' fathers practiced their swordsmanship in mock duels, which were more about dance than combat. And women with long braids washing clothes in the river, providing inspiring colorful insults to their husbands when their beloveds' asses fell into the mud. And praises when they outwitted their opponents with sword or acrobatics. And elders arguing politics with their rock hard asses glued to tree stumps, debating as to whether the Orthodox Christian Cossacks should side with the Czar and Imperialists in the new revolution coming up, or the 'godless Communists'. Whose ideology and activities were far more Christ-like and Christian than that of the old Aristocratic order that still treated commoners, and Cossacks who were not powerful enough, like serfs.

My eyes were kept hostage by other things. The field was plowed with symmetrical rows, sprouting plants designed to feed humans rather than free grazing livestock. And there were tractors with fresh dirt on their rotors instead of plows usually pulled by horses or, on occasion, Cossack men or women who had committed too many transgressions against their community. Those ancient plows, which had sustained humans and animals for centuries, had been broken into unusable debris, their rusted elements blending in with the dirt. And there were dragons on the unfarmed regions of the meadow, eating holes into the earth with their extended mouths, surrounded by black soot.

"Oil," Stefan explained to me regarding the rigs. "Which we do need, so that we can fuel trucks, tractors, and carts so that no one has to put any one of your equine brethren into harness, ever again!"

"And the streets will smell of black soot, and the sky can become a lovely shade of grey," I felt like saying. "And those streets instead of having occasional piles of droppings from our asses will be 'graced' by fecal material from people who can't afford to live in houses? People who forgot that if you put any of OUR horse manure onto any arid land, it will turn even sand into a soil enriched garden?" My still not completely repaired shoulder from being overused in the military harness, and the memory of seeing my equine Comrades develop sweeny so bad that they had to be turned into meat came to mind. But, looking at the house Stefan was bringing me to put an even more toxic aroma into my nostrils. It was nothing that I could recall biologically, but I feared that I would be able to define it very very soon.

The walls of the house were constructed of freshly painted wood, brown with white trimmings around the windows. Appliances requiring electricity were in every corner of the recently built dwelling: lamps, stoves, and a machine that was used for washing clothes. The sink in the kitchen featured water coming out of a pipe when the 'woman of the house' pushed the lever up and down. Her artificially curled blonde hair was neatly trimmed to just below her shoulders. Her dress was red, its hem falling just below the knee. Her size 6 feet were adorned with French-made pumps rather than Cossack-crafted boots. Stefan, still mounted, knocked three times on the kitchen window. "I'm home, Svetlana! My love!" he declared, whipping his tall Cossack hat in the air.

"Yes, I can see that," his wife impersonally spat out from the side of her mouth, having seen us through the reflection in the mirror as she continued to wash dishes made of China rather than hand-flattened metal or clay.

"And I brought a friend with me," Stefan exclaimed with glee, more as a boy half his age than a man who had been, from his perspective anyway, halfway around the world since enlisting in the Army.

"As I can also see, my dear Stefan," her reply, smiling to our reflection in the mirror rather than to us.

"And I'm stationed here indefinitely, as a decorated Sergeant about to be promoted to…Lieutenant!" he boasted. He pulled out the officer insignia from his breast pocket that he was permitted to sew onto his uniform after arriving at his 'post', placing it on his shoulders, securing it with gum.

"So, I've heard," Svetlana said. She finally turned to us, her smile becoming more 'classy' than common.

"I'm waiting for other soldiers to command, and, so I'm told, no one to command me! Imagine that! A Don River Cossack commanding White Russians from Moscow, Petersburg, and Minsk!" he boasted. "Can you imagine that!?"

"Yes, I think I can," she replied with an all-knowing nod of her rounded chin and beautiful face. "Suppose that when life gives us what we want, we need to honor its request," she said, after which she approached the window. Stefan leaped off my back and gave her an enthusiastic over-the-top hug, which she received with civility and grace. She kissed him on the lips, then pulled back. She sniffed the air and winced her thin, perfectly shaped nose, finding the aroma near Stefan distasteful. Then she sampled the air near me, pulling her dainty teeth backward into an even more disgruntled expression.

"I know, we both have been on the road for a long time, and a husband should greet his wife with a more presentable aromatic presence," Stefan said to his wife. A wife who had no wedding ring on her finger. The one on Stefan's right hand was still on so tightly that it had penetrated into the bone.

Before I could nudge Stefan's puppy-love eyes away from Svetlana's deceptive ocular portholes and towards her ringless right hand, the new 'Commander's' wife gave me a dirty look. The kind that said 'do what I say or it's the butcher for your flesh and the glue factory for your hoofs'. Knowing that she had the authority to make such happen, I nudged her left hand, trying to gain her affection. Then her right, so that Stefan could notice that she had declared herself 'unmarried' in his absence.

"We found each other," Stefan said by way of explanation regarding me. "His name is Achilles. He is fluent in Austrian German, Continental Italian, Cossack

Ukrainian, and even Russian," he boasted. "And I think he likes you."

"Yes, I think he can be…useful," she replied, pretending to like me.

What kind of useful, I was not sure of. But I knew I had to be useful to Stefan. Part of my job of being assigned to look after him by my bosses, who, well, I will tell you more about later.

"But in the meantime," Sventlana said with a welcoming smile, "Our children will be pleased to see you! They are very proud of you, you know."

"As I am proud of them," Stefan replied. "As they know."

"Which they need to be reminded of, Stefan?" came from Svetlana. They were the first honest words to come out of her angelic lips.

# CHAPTER 5

Svetlana requested that Stefan bathe before supper. After looking inside the bed he would finally share with his wife, he asked if she had a bathtub he could fill with hot water. She pointed to the river, saying to her husband, with a warm smile, "There is more water in the river than in my bathtub, and it's a lot colder, which is good for your health and a remedy for inappropriate urges you may be thinking about. And besides, that's what your ancestors did after coming home victoriously from a War. With…how much compensation are you getting as a Sergeant, and how much will you get paid as a Lieutenant?"

"The honor of serving the Lord through serving more of His people," Stefan replied with pride.

Even a dog, after being kicked in the head by a horse, would have picked up the true meaning of Svetlana's words. But it was the smile she put on her face that Stefan chose to fix upon as he led me to the river. And, to be fair, Svetlana had probably been in love with Stefan in SOME way. Until she saw that he was more easily pitied than loved or understood. Why else would she have two children with him?

Stefan spoke to me about them often, recalling who they were when he departed to fight in the War that would keep them safe, secure, and happy. Sasha, a strapping lad of 15 years and almost as much height as Stefan. And Tanya, a young woman of 13 years who danced more than walked or ran when moving from the barn to the house. Or from the house to any other house.

Those offspring bearing Stefan's name appeared, dropped off by an Asian driver, in a car. Unlike when Stefan left, their clothing was clean, containing no holes, and not smelling of farm or wild animals. They looked at Stefan as if he were from another planet.

Stefan brought his children into a three-person hug, their arms rigidly on their upper legs. He kissed them both on the cheek. "I know, it's been three long years. But I thought of you every day. And if you don't recognize me, well, the War changes everyone on the inside and the outside," he said by way of explanation.

"Yes, I heard," Tanya said, averting her eyes.

"And as I read, in the uncensored books in the library," Sasha added, looking at and into Stefan's life, tired but still wide open ocular portholes. "And the soldiers who ran away from the war, or were lucky enough to have an injury that justified their discharge."

"Who really weren't able to carry a weapon, or charge at the Huns' line," Stefan's brother Andrei said as he limped his way from the woods, a snared rabbit flung over his shoulder. "I really wanted to enlist when you did in 1914, Stefan, but…" he pointed to his left leg. "The doctors say it's incurable."

"Which THIS boy, no MAN, will be able to make functional again!" Stefan said, trapping his 15-year-old son in an even tighter bear hug. A son who looked more like Stefan's brother than Stefan himself. "When Sasha becomes the youngest doctor on the Steppes, he will undo whatever that accident did to your leg, Andre, and right arm three years ago. He's still getting great grades toward that end," Stefan said to his non-biological son. "Right? he continued, looking at the lad with more pride than in his voice than I ever heard from him, or any other human."

"I'm getting the best grades that I can buy or steal," Sasha replied to his father, who pulled back his head in something resembling shock. "A joke, of course," the lad smiled into his father's still, village idiot brain, after which he looked at his sister. "Right, Tanya?"

"Of course. Sasha is to be the best medical scientist in Ukraine. My fate and calling are to become the best dancer." Tanya assured her (due to her resembling Andre more than Stefan), non-biological dad. "A dancer who, of course, shares the stage with everyone else instead of hogging it all for herself, because, as you, and Mama taught us…"

"Great work only happens when you are humble, giving more than you take," father and daughter said, in unison.

"And, as every Cossack knows or should know," Andrei interjected. "Great work always requires everyone giving according to their abilities and taking ONLY according to their needs. According to the Communists."

"Who, I know, most Cossacks refuse to join," Stefan said. "Or maybe will join when this War is over. On their own terms. Because, as we know, you can lead an Islamic Cossack to vodka, you can't make him drink it."

Stefan's son, daughter, and brother put forced smiles on their faces, chuckling with strained voices. Stefan, of course, believed their laughter at his joke was real. And so did I, until I noted Andrei placing his crutch over his shoulder and trotting towards the town tavern as sound as any newborn colt or well-conditioned stallion.

# CHAPTER 6

The newest and busiest business in Iankovia was a set of peers at the river, which had been turned into a harbor. Or as I remember seeing on my many boat journeys that made life easy for the feet, but hard on the belly and putrid for the nostrils for fellow transported equines, and humans, a port. "You should have seen it in the old days, just…well two and a half long years and fifteen hundred and ten four and two legged patients I stitched up ago," Stefan related to me as he did his daily 'inspection' of the town on my back. "Furs and meat from old and sick animals we hunted or slaughtered to end their suffering, and wheat that grew in our rich soil would go out to cities where people had forgotten how to hunt and didn't own land to grow food." He leaned back, arching his back as if to boast the accomplishments that were now rewarded by the medals on his uniform, given to him by Ivanov. And on top of that, he was now an officer who still had no Sergeants, Corporals, or Privates to command, or look after, or be talked back to. Surrendering his current sense of time and place to the river as it captured his gaze yet again, he continued. "When the wind was good, we used a sail. When the wind was hiding, or wanted to work against us, we rowed our solid hand

hand-built wooden boats to where our goods were supposed to go. Yes, we complained about our muscles hurting, but it made us stronger. All in the service of others, who give according to our abilities, and take according to our needs, and NOT our or their wants." He then recited some idealistic words from the Communist Manifesto, in original German, sharing its magic with a smile as he patted my neck.

Though Stefan's German was still poorly accented, missing the articles which are part of the language of Marx and Engels but not in his own Slavic tongue, they did make sense to me. I let his sincerity, optimism, and firm trust in right ruling over might come into me. "Yes, our Motherland, Russia, is our Master, and it is our honor to serve her during these perilous times," he said to me in Ukrainian, a tongue I had become functionally fluent in, at least as a listener, in a voice that was kind and gentle. Until we, I anyway, heard Austrian German from the skipper of an incoming oversized steel boat driven by an engine, directing his crew. As soon as he was within hearing range of Slavic workers on shore, he commanded Ilya Vladivich, a one-armed Ukrainian foreman, to prepare the dock for his landing in Ukrainian.

Ilya was a fellow Cossack and boyhood friend of Stefan, who, according to a one-way conversation Stefan had with me earlier that day, had been honorably discharged from the Imperial Russian Army. Illya had cut off his Cossack warlock and now had grown a 'respectable' worker's disheveled mop of hair on his head, with a now neatly trimmed rather than boldly displayed overgrown mustache. Illya asked the Captain who he was, in German.

"Someone who is paying your boss with this!" the Austrian Captain growled at Ilya in Ukrainian, as he pulled out a fistful of money, waving it in the air. Deutschmarks, Rubles, Dollars, and Pounds. "And if you do it faster, this is a personal tip!" He pulled opened his weather-beaten civilian coat, revealing an Austrian Army uniform under it, something the 'enemy' did so that they would not be shot as a spy when stepping 'outside' of the lines, showing Iliya even more currency, waving it like a carrot. "For everything you have in that wagon!" The captain commanded, pointing to an overloaded cart at the dock covered with a tarp. "And already loaded into that other ship," he said of a smaller unmanned boat docked next to his bearing a Russian flag, being loaded up with grain, meat, and more importantly, barrels of oil. "And I have even more money for your crew," the Austrian Captain said regarding the two armed workers who had stopped working.

"But," Ilya protested. "The crew for that other ship is in the tavern, and if they come back and find out that I didn't deliver what they came for."

"So, you give them more vodka, more food, and more women to play with. And when they sober up and, maybe shower, you will give them this!" he continued throwing Iliya a bag of money. Looking at the amount inside, Iliya threw the Captain's 'civilian merchant' a rope. The engine on the Austrian 'merchant ship' was silenced, its bow pulled into the pole. Its deck was filled with alacrity with the most recent delivery of goods that had arrived at the port, as well as the lion's share of the cargo in the Russian ship by Slavic dock hands who were thrown small but still ample bags of coin by the Captain.

"But," Illya asked the Austrian Captain, as his 'loyal' fellow Slavs men ran over him while obeying their new foreman. "What will I tell the Russian soldiers who I'm supposed to give this to when they discover that we under delivered to them?"

"Or as your boss knows, it may not be Russian soldiers at all. Or perhaps Russian soldiers who maybe have become deserters, Reds, or...one of us?" the Captain proposed. "Or pirates in the service of our wives and children at home, or our mistresses and adopted offspring in other lands? It's every MAN for himself. Every MAN if he is going to take care of his family, or himself, has to now be a pirate who cares for no one who isn't family, God help us," He crossed himself in a manner of the Catholics, differently than the Eastern Orthodox with respect to the right vs the left shoulder being touched first.

"And what do we tell God when we face our final judgement?" Iliya challenged.

"For Father Basili," the Austrian Captain said, sneaking into Iliya's pocket a fistful of mixed currency. "And as for God, we tell the Almighty whatever He wants to hear. Through, if necessary, we hire His most valued intermediaries, which of course are..."

"...Jewish lawyers," Both men said in unison, sharing a joke, Vision and a new agenda for a new century.

With that, Iliya joined in the loading operation, the Austrian cruiser sinking three feet deeper into the water with barrels of oil destined for destination points to be determined. Points no doubt where there would be another transaction which would profit neither Czar nor Kaiser, Emperor nor peasants. Peasants who, along with many others, were becoming homeless, limbless, and lifeless in the service of God and Country.

"Did you hear any of that?" I tried to communicate to Stefan, in horse language, then in the human voice I once had before taking on my current life form.' He merely looked on at the loaded Austrian ship leaving with the oil and other booty, a Russian flag hoisted on its mast, which he saluted after he prodded me forward, closer to the dock.

"We have to do something about this!?" I blasted out through engorged nostrils. "YOU have to do something about this. Find this 'boss pirate'. And..."

My voice was shut down by the Austrian Army Officer, or perhaps German Pirate Captain, looking at me. He ran his index finger across his neck. Then, while still staring at me, he tapped the handle of the revolver strapped to his fat waist, giving me the option as to how I would be released from my present body so I could use, or abuse, another one should I get in his way. But he seemed to recognize me as his prize horse who deserted not only himself, but the Army I was conscripted to join.

Thinking with my feet, as we horses are said to do, I jolted to the left and thunder bolted Stefan back to town, toward and into the tavern where the (most probably anyway) REAL Russian ship operators were being 'entertained' while the goods they were supposed to bring back to the front were being sent, most probably, to the enemy.

# CHAPTER 7

Faking being scared of a wolf in the woods, I detoured Stefan towards the tavern, the last known whereabouts of the Russian soldiers who were, or maybe now had been, members of his Army charged with bringing goods back to their commanders from Iankovia. It took longer than I thought. Part of the reason for such was that I myself got lost amidst the wagons and trucks carting large barrels of crude 'black gold' from what used to be farm fields to the docks. And some of the delay was due to Stefan himself, who tried to pull me back to the river. It was the first real argument I had with Stefan, but one I could not lose for either of us. Or for the horses that were now being overworked, hauling wagonloads of crude oil rather than being given a break due to the emergence of trucks and mechanized tractors.

By the time we finally arrived at the village tavern, Stefan had exhausted all of expletives he knew in at least five languages, damning me and the beasts he thought were causing me to spook. I reared up, landing his ass as close to a pile of straw bails as I could. Then, I nudged at the door, finding it locked, a 'closed for lunch' sign on it. With a swift kick nearly as intense as I gave the Austrian Captain before I resigned my commission in his Army, I kicked the door open and entered, on my own accord, bringing Stefan with me, then dumping him on his ass. Behind the door was none other than Andrei, Stefan's brother, fresh blood on his apron. "That's it for you!'" Andrei yelled as he aimed his sawed-off shotgun at my head.

"No!" Stefan screamed back, kicking the business end of the weapon upward. It fired into the roof of the establishment, causing the chandelier to crash to the floor. I lingered to see what the two brothers would do with, for, or to each other. "What's with the blood?" Stefan asked.

"An accident in the kitchen," Andrei replied. "We have it under control."

"And 'we' is who?" Stefan…yes…pressed.

Andrei pulled back his lips, his smile warm and supportive. "Someone you don't need to know about. And don't want to know, little brother," he continued, bringing Stefan into a hug. "And as for your equine friend there," he said as I remained in the vestibule of the establishment.

"And as for whose blood is on the floor?" Stefan asked, noting several piles of bright red fluid, scrapings of them oozing in from the kitchen and out the back door.

"Some butchering had to be done in the dining room," the explanation. "And the meat is… processed."

Amidst the two blood pockets were buttons from enlisted men in the Czar's army and a broken insignia from a Russian Lieutenant's uniform. I pushed Stefan towards them, causing him to fall down to be sure he would see them as he got up.

"What's this?" Stefan asked politely, holding the buttons and insignia in his still-uninjured hand.

"Something that has been taken care of," Andrei said as he limped towards his brother, then lifted him up off the floor. "And there is something that you, and that horse of yours, should know. A proverb that has served us all very well."

"Which is?" Stefan inquired.

"He who…well…" Andrei clapped his hands together, summoning to the customer lacking tavern drinking and dining room his wife Svetlana, his son Sasha, his daughter Tanya, and no less than five underdressed young women he didn't recognize. And a band of gypsies bearing musical instruments and bloody boots. "All together now!" he announced.

"He who asks too many questions gets too many answers!" the congregation declared, after which the gypsies struck a folk tune from Stefan's youth. The five whores, two of which Stefan did recognize, sang in three-part harmony to the song of celebration. Tanya's feet absorbed the music, inspiring a dance that everyone joined in. Including Andrei, whose gimped feet has no shortage of vitality, strength and musicality, most particularly when he grabbed hold of his most favored partner in dance, Svetlana, who he kissed passionately on the lips. The vision of such entered Stefan's eyes. But before it could enter his brain one of the whores who had no doubt 'pleasured' the Russian soldiers with a few minutes of earthly carnal bliss before being given free 'you dare not decline this offer' tickets to enter Heaven or Purgatory, pulled Stefan into the dance. Then his angelic, purer than any other virgin daughter, Tanya, whose dress was spotted with blood and whose crotch smelled like fresh semen, cut in, requesting a private dance with her father. As an obedient 'protector of the people,' Stefan honored her wishes, or had none of his own left. He let her do all the thinking and the dancing, leading with every step of her slender ballerina feet and lily white arms.

Stefan's thoughts faded into a blank stare. Finally, his wall of idealism was in the first stage of being shattered with knowledge he, maybe, could comprehend. An understanding of the world as it is.

Burley, well-fed dock workers entered the establishment, with their fists and pockets flushed with money, showing it off to Andrei. "Your best vodka!" one of them said. "And your best women?" another one demanded, showing off his ill-gotten booty. "And not your wife or daughter this time!" a third requested. "And some equine stew," a fourth said after smelling my sweat, finding it offensive. "To add to the two-legged meat you already put into the daily special," a fifth added.

So that I would still be around to help him ride into it as an effective agent of Truth and effective compassion, I backed away, then ran into the woods. Two of the newly arrived burly male patrons bearing sabres and pistols ran after me. I couldn't see what Stefan saw about my demise. Of course, he would have intervened if he knew I was in danger. Such was my hope anyway.

# CHAPTER 8

I needed some time alone, so I hid from every living thing except the flies, frogs, foxes, and whatever wild geese that had decided to come home to mate and lay their eggs. They all had their conflicting purpose and personal agendas, of course. Predators had to eat prey to stay alive, and one way or another, all of the prey fed on something lower on the food chain.

There was some healing I had to do myself as well. A villager's bullet grazed me in the left hip, and a wolf decided that God had created me to be meat for his family, leaving claw marks on my neck prior to me kicking him in the teeth. It was payback, of course, perhaps for having been a skilled marksman and hunter in my last body possession. And a successful one at that, as measured by wealth seeking and valuing humans anyway.

But I was also a self-taught philosopher, having attended my own university after learning how to read and finding out I enjoyed it. While munching on a patch of grass between piles of forage which had been blackened by oil, my thoughts went to Socrates., who after his state mandated suicide perhaps did come back as a ghost to instruct his favorite student, Plato, to quote what he had said while alive and to do it accurately. The ghost of the bodiless Athenian professor in the school of Life lamented that he never wrote down his messages to the world, due to his being dyslexic. Whether Socrates' inability to read or write was a blessing or a curse, that was another matter. But some things that came out of his ass, or mouth, came to my mind as I felt a need to do something more with a new body.

I shared my thoughts with a field mouse whose brain seemed to be big for its body size. Whether said rodent was using his brain to secure a more influential incarnation after his inevitable demise by foxes, hounds, or annoyed horses, I didn't know. But he or, as I suspected, as much as possible, she was a good listener.

"So, it is said that ignorance is the sole reason for cruelty. Is that not so?" I telepathed to the rodents in the manner that Socrates invited open dialog with his students, friends, or anyone in the streets who would listen to him.

With her big eyes, she winked and said, 'Yes,' to that Socratic quote.

"And by inference, is it not so that intelligence inevitably produces compassion?" I inquired of the mouse.

"She said 'yes' to that with a chirp and a nod.

"But!" I continued, feeling a new thought, a new idea, a practical ideal entering my cerebral cortex courtesy of the third brain that had emerged between me and the rodent. Something that happened with many animals in my current life form, and, on special moments anyway, even with less cerebrally effective creatures such as Stefan. A human who had magical skills as a healer of disease and traumatized biological flesh, who, by logic anyway, might one day be a healer of the human mind who would enlighten, inspire, and liberate the collective human soul.

I held on to this new idea floating in my mind, trying to grab it, capture it and own it before it slipped away into the ethers, as innovative thoughts so often do, for reasons probably based in some way the brain was designed so that it would not become 'too big for its britches'. Finally, I gave voice to it, with my eyes, and with 'horse speak,' both of which my new rodent 'girlfriend' seemed to be interested in. "If intelligence produces compassion, is it intelligence with regard to how the world SHOULD BE or intelligence regarding the world as it IS, which is the kind of intelligence that leads to EFFECTIVE compassion?" I offered for assessment.

I proposed to her, myself and the third brain floating around us (which some say is God, as when two or more of you are gathered in my name, I'm there also) the idea that intelligence of an idealist living in or aspiring to a 'Higher Planc' of consciousness produces the most effective brand of compassion. The mouse, who seemed more like Aspasia, Socrates' Platonic courtesan mistress rather than his bitchy, unappreciative, social climbing wife, shook her head with a 'no'. When proposing that being a cynic, who sees all the dirt in the world and none of the virtue humans stumble into, makes one a channel for maximal effective compassion, she nodded an assuring 'yes'. But with a coda to that finale.

"Yes, I know," I replied, feeling then recognizing that thought and strategy. "One has to be a well-informed cynic who still has hope that there IS virtue, beauty, and love as the ultimate goal. And that the destiny for all creatures, including humans, is to experience and be channels for… Goodness."

'Aspasia', as I named her, brought me some berries, laying them in front of my mouth. I smelled them, recalling portions of a distant memory. When I started to help myself to the sweet-tasting forage, she bit my face.

"Yes," I said to her, the pieces of that memory pieced together. "Too much of a good and needed thing can cause more problems than cures," I thought, and gave voice to.

Indeed, these berries were the ones I ate when a stupid and, yes, happy because of such, human before I had to switch bodies. "Maybe there is something in these berries that fits better into Stefan's biology than mine?" I said. "Or yours?" I asked Aspasia.

She said yes in many different animal and human languages, as I heard it anyway. Then ran away, leaving me the responsibility, and perhaps glory, of turning a pathological idealist savant 'village idiot' who provides ridicule, entertainment, and services to the flesh into something more effective. Without, of course, the protection conferred by God from physical harm or mental anguish. After all, the 'Heavenly Father' protects fools, drunks, and idealists who saw every circle of hell on earth as a subdivision of Heaven. But not truth-seeking questioners. The price of eating the tree of knowledge in the garden of Eden, according to the fables humans are taught at an early age, which, truth be told, seldom leaves the belief systems they carry to the grave in old age. And by 'coincidence,' these apple-tasting berries I indulged in by 'coincidence' still grew in Iankovia, one of the many towns in isolated areas in isolated countries which at one time or another were 'Edens.'

# CHAPTER 9

It wasn't hard to find scientifica fructum afferentem (as it was called in my time anyway) around Iankovia. Just look around where the oil rigs that were not in commission have been dismantled or turned into distilleries. But barely one in ten twigs bore the apple-tasting berry now. And ingestion of three 'swallowfuls' from the low growing bush that disguised itself as a weed smelling of skunk produced no more than a fourth of its usual effect on the 'assessment of raw reality' machine between the ears, on me or (as I was painfully able to assess it) the other 'subhuman; creatures around me.

Who was eating the herb that lowered activity in the 'feeling' portion of the brain and activated it in the 'seeing as it really is' centers? Or what environmental toxin was driving scientifica fructum afferentem into extinction, modifying some of the plants into something as ineffective as the apples growing from a tree that sprouted fruits above our heads? I didn't know. But this now necessary experiment involving the 'more heart than brains' Cossack who was on my back 6 hours a day had to be launched. The fate of Stefan's village, the world around it, and the, as I saw it anyway, continuing life experiments of the self-interest driven creatures who had two, four, six, or no legs inhabiting this planet depended on Stefan dining on the appropriate dose of scientifica.

"So, when I ask what kind of grass you want to eat, you come here to where it's low lying brown instead of high growing green?" Stefan said to me on a half cloudy and half sunny day in the oil fields after I obeyed HIS travel route on the daily inspection of the town he was supposed to administer. For weeks, he had found nothing out of order anywhere. And believed every lie, be it white or black, he was told by his well-fed and (for appearances' sake to outsiders) poorly clothed 'Comrade Citizens.' "I don't know what you want to eat, but you know best, I suppose," he continued to me as his eyelids grew heavy, and I ate whatever grass I could get that wasn't coated with oil or stained with 'scientifica' berry juice.

Stefan faded into another one of his ten-second 'sleeps', the smile on his face saying that he was dreaming about something magnificent and, in his mind, inevitable. 'In the Heavenly Father's time,' of course. That Heavenly Father being God, or perhaps his new Prophet, Vladimir Lenin. Stefan really did believe that the Bolshevik leader was not really an atheist, but someone who was secretly working with the Eastern Orthodox Church with the aim of infusing more humanistic Spirituality than traditional Theology into its mandates. "Yes, Comrade Lenin, you are right about that, right about that, right about that..." Stefan periodically muttered more than usually on this trip to the woods when reading Das Kapital and the Communist

Manifesto. Of course, if one were a true Christian or Cossack, you were not allowed to be a Communist. According to most of the Christians, Cossacks, or Communists I had met, or had the 'pleasure' of being a beast of burden to.

Stefan's smile during his dream naps was bigger than normal today, and he smelt of alcohol today more than most days, along with something else I couldn't identify. Of course, he, knowingly anyway, never drank anything that came from a distillery. Someone was feeding him 'happy juice' without his knowing it, most likely. Something those on top who 'know' do to, or for, those on the bottom who 'don't 'know. Another 'constant' that kept the world going so that it would keep the 'good ship earth' sailing in waters that, more than ever now, were plagued with icebergs of many varieties and appearances. Yes, it was time that SOMEone did something about the world, and…the Stefans.

Stefan maintained a loose rein on me as it was 'ice cream time'. That half hour a day when he allowed me to eat the grass I wanted to, while I decided on whether I would go right or left, walk on or linger, look out into the woods or point my ears to the ground.

My nose smelt the scientifica plants in abundance amidst weeds, which were now spouting burdock, thus keeping humans and most animals away from the 'forbidden plant'. Below my feet, I felt vibration from the earth. An electrical jolt of sorts, which increased in intensity as I moved along to the center of the 'power spot'.

This one is NOT outlined by a circle of rocks, as was the case with most 'medicine wheels.'

I recalled with glee and excitement times of old when lightning from the sky shook the stagnant consciousness of common earth-bound creatures who walked on four legs into being… different. Different than their friends, family, and even mentors. Turning them into creatures who could teach so much and who, as a reward for that curse and blessing, would be actively ignored for the rest of their lives. But that was then, and this was now. An evolving 'now.' With an unevolved Stefan on my back who took in a deep breath, looked up to the sky, then said, as he patted my back, "Is it not a great thing that God made the world so great and wonderful! And left us with the most important job of all! To celebrate all of the goodness around us!"

I rolled my eyes once again, in the manner of a human soul utilizing an equine body, Stefan not seeing it, of course. I treated myself to vicariously enjoying the wide, contented, happy smile on Stefan's face. Something he would never experience again, according to my experience and knowledge of what would happen to and for him.

I allowed him one last breath of putrid petroleum infused air tinged with the scent of the flowers from weeds that flourished with the newly transformed profitable ground that he considered heavenly, then kicked my rear fetlocks up above my head, tossing his ass into the air. Then I turned abruptly to the left. Then rolled into his back, directing his fall so that it would preserve his head but make his face land into a collection of ripe, bright red scientific berries growing in the middle of what probably at one time was, or maybe in the future would be, a medicine wheel. A power spot. At least one 'gulpful' of 'scientifica' found its way into his open mouth. An unexpected jolt of felt but not seen lightning from the earth penetrated into his belly, sending jolts of shakes up his spine and down into his toes.

"Ah!!" Stefan moaned in pain as no less than ten waves of electrification went up and down his spine, his eyelids shut hard, maybe due to lightning from the earth, or maybe from some devise that was built by hands other than Mother Nature buried in the ground. I feared that if the latter was the case, I had stumbled onto someone else's experiment, which had an aim different than the one assigned to me.

I edged my way towards Stefan, moving my snout to push him away from the jolt, which seemed to be more powerful than the one I anticipated. But he declined and refused my instruction. "Ahhh!!!!" he said by way of explanation, the grimace on his lips turning into a shit eating grin of discovery. His eyes are open wide. He assured me that 'the light coming in is setting fire to my (his) brain'. He cleaned the excess berry fragments from his face with his finger and ingested them. "Mmmmm." He said with delight. 'Mmmm, ' he exclaimed as he helped himself to the lion's share of the crushed berries on the ground, finding them as tasty to the palate as it was enriching to his belly and brain. "And" he exclaimed as he ingested the remainder of the fruit on the low-lying bush I had chosen for him.

I tried to stop him from dining on an adjacent bush which was would have turned his first scientifica meal into into a glutinous orgy. This time, by nudging his hand, asking to share in the feast. He complied, thankfully. "Mmm...." he kept saying to himself, and me, regarding the taste of the residual fruit lingering on his lips and hands. With smiles that somehow made his aura, something which I didn't think I imagined this time, become larger and whiter. Then it emerged into rhythmic fire.

Upon holding the last berry in his hand, the joy of discovery on his face turned into a grimace of concern. "Mmmm,' Stefan said reflectively, nodding his head, then scratching his hairless chin in a professorial manner, something he had never done. After several 'hmmms' of internal reflection, seeing things behind the blank stares in his eyes that were images that only he could see, a wall was put up against them, to me anyway, he looked up to the sky. 'Hmmm,' he said to the God in the sky whom he always trusted, liked, and loved. "Hmm?" he continued, asking the Divinity, picking up a bone from a child near the power spot that I had not seen. A cancerous bone, covered with black spurs and cracks, exposing foul-smelling marrow.

"Hmm...' he said to the bone, trying to ascertain the significance of such. "Why?" he asked God the Father, holding it up. "An eight-year-old child! Why?" He waited for an answer. "Of course, because it was your Will, you sadistic bastard. Who...." He finally said. He looked to me, "doesn't know he is a sadist or....maybe doesn't exist at all," he assured me. "But we do exist, and have to keep on living," the idealistic boy whom I had been training said to me as a mature man. A good man, by the way he seemed, was according in the gentle yet firm way he adjusted my bridle. A determined one, as assessed by the abrupt, firm, and necessary tightening of the girth securing the saddle. An effective one, I hoped, as he dumped his ass on my tired back, dispassionately, without song and without explanation, directing our movements back to town.

# CHAPTER 10

That traditional victory Cossack song, 'The Cossack Rode Beyond the Danube', reached our ears from the village square long before we saw any buildings. It was nothing unusual. But what was unusual was that it was sung by men, women, and children. "What are they celebrating?" I asked myself out loud with whatever inflections in the mouth and tongue a horse can do.

"A dream that will become a nightmare soon enough," Stefan answered, reading my thoughts. Something he was not able to do in his pre-scientific state so clearly and literally. "It is true and will be reality, despite what the newspaper the wind 'coincidently' blew into my face, and yours, says."

"But," I projected to him in 'horse talk' which he was able to understand. "You read the headlines in those newspapers that somehow reached the general store, then were surrendered to the wind, as clearly as I did. The Czar is stepping down from the throne without anyone firing a shot, and the Socialist Mensheviks are designing a democratic government that serves rather than exploits the people."

"Yes, while they still intend not to pull out of the War with the Austrians and Germans, a war to keep the Kings, Kaisers, and Capitalists in power at the expense of their people," Stefan related to me. "Anyone with any horse or common human sense should know that, but tragically, don't. Or choose to stay ignorant about it because it is more profitable and socially comfortable to do so. And as for democracy, Socrates was put to death by a show of hands for corrupting the youth, and that same assembly erected a statue in his honor two weeks later."

I halted my forward progress, locking my legs in place. "My still, I think, good friend Stefan, I thought that you welcomed the Socialists taking power. Socialists who believe in God and the power of basic goodness, like you, still believe in God," I was about to say.

"Like I DID!" Stefan related to me, prior to giving voice to that thought, ashamed of his past ignorance of the way things really were. "And those idiots and assholes in town, and occupying the house I still call home, do. But some things have to be corrected, NOW! Now that I'm just another asshole, but not an idiot anymore!" he growled, appended by kicking my groin with the spurs he normally only used on reluctant horses, and with the most gentle of touches. "I remind you that I'm the head asshole here!" he added, holding up a stick he was prepared to use as a whip. "Now. MOVE!" he commanded me, as if I were an idiot. Maybe I was. Or had to be, for what was to happen.

I edged ahead at a walk, then, at Stefan's 'all business and no pleasure or passion' vocal command, at a trot.

When we arrived at the village square, it was a festive occasion. I had never seen such wide, heartfelt smiles on humans. The air smelled of four varieties of freshly cooked meat, three times that number of legumes, and of course vodka. "Come, my brother, join the feast!" Andrei, the head chef, exclaimed.

"No, join the dance, Papa!" Stefan's daughter Tanya insisted as she danced her way around me in circles. "And your horse, too!" she added. "I heard about how you and he danced the Austrians into submission at the front! Putting a mirror in their faces so looked inside themselves and laid down their arms."

"Yes, I suppose we did," I reminded Stefan. "That got us sent here, walking on our feet instead of being wheeled in as corpses."

"It was a different time, different place, and…" Stefan said to Tanya, giving the appearance of ignoring me. He sniffed the air. "What is that smell?" he intuited.

"Food, drink, happiness?" Tanya answered, still dancing.

"And gratitude to the Lord," came from behind us as Father Basili approached. With the same odor on him as was lingering on Stefan's daughter.

Yes, it was the aroma of ejaculate. Sperm juice. Which, to my equine olfactory senses, was all alike no matter what man it came from. But Stefan sensed, intuited, and somehow knew something different. Or maybe it was something he saw in the way the good 50-year-old Holy Father with the best-fed belly and finest clothes in the village danced with the soon-to-be 'sent to Moscow as a star dancer' Tanya that cued him into it. An assessment of 'data' when he had attended Mass that finally registered in the thinking rather than believing portion of his now (according to some measures anyway) 'advanced' brain.

"Come, join us in the dance, Papa!" Tanya beckoned to Stefan, yet again. 'You deserve some happiness!"

Stefan dismounted. A still limping Andrei approached him, offering to take the reins. "The next time I smell horsemeat in your stew, it will be your genuinely broken leg that winds up in the cooking pot," Stefan whispered to his draft dodging brother. "And if there is any more human meat in your delicacies that I don't approve of first, as Commandant of town, your testicles, eyeballs, and tongue will become the delicacies that are sent out of here for sale. Got it?"

Andrei DID 'get it.' He handled me with the utmost respect, gentleness and fear. Yes, I did take advantage of such by nibbling at his pants and shirt, and taking all of the carrots and apples in his pockets, and leaving a large hole exposing his naked ass in my wake.

Stefan, sporting a shit eating grin on his (as assessed only by the truly blind, which now included everybody else) 'happy' face joined the now circle dance, villagers linking arms and hearts. He whispered into the Good Father's ear something. That sounded, and with my lip-reading eyes, looked like 'I know you have your own private secretary and the occasionally sexually confused altar boy to give you pleasures, but even if my daughter comes to you for special favors with your contacts in Kiev, you will refuse her.' I can't swear to that being the exact words, but after Stefan nodded in satisfaction when the Good Father lowered his eyes when a shocked Tanya looked at him. Stefan added something else to his new directives to Father Basili, which encouraged him to leave the dance, spinning his way to a stoop, then emptying the contents of his pants pockets into the collection box. Stefan yelled out something to him in Greek, which I didn't understand. It must have meant 'and the rest of what you stole from these people and others', appended by Stefan, gently placing his fingers on the handle of his revolver between 'twirls' with his daughter. The Good Father emptied the remainder of coins, jewels, and paper money that was in his many deep pockets, then his shirt and cross into the collection pot. He then headed off into the woods, alone, shuffling his feet, his arched back now hunched in despair. No one followed him.

The dancers released their hold on each other, each couple or single dancer doing their own steps.

"One down, many more to go," Stefan said to himself, and I think to myself, with a satisfied voice and dispassionate smile as he looked at the priest who was not in his employ but rather in the service of himself. This time, his daughter heard him.

"What did you say, Papa?" Tanya asked, after which she displayed her skill as a dancer with acrobatics that impressed the men in the village. Such intimidated her fellow teenagers 'girlfriends into attempting to do the same, resulting in them stumbling onto each other, and their eyerolling dancing partners.

"You SHARE the stage with others, and don't take it all for yourself," Stefan said, picking up his daughter's hand as she reached it out to him. "Or, accidents of lack of talent or lack of appropriate professional contacts can come your way." With a twist of her arm that only I could see, Stefan catapulted his star dancing daughter into a fall that forced her into a roll that muddied her clean white, and sperm smelling dress. Appended by her clean lily white face landing in a pile of horse shit. My shit, interestingly enough. The musicians stopped playing. The gourmands stopped eating. The merchant oil and who knows what else 'buyers' from foreign lands, not identified by their commoner clothing (most of them having over their unidentified military tunics under them), stopped chatting in their native tongues.

Tanya's subordinate girlfriends, her 'back up dancers' as Stefan recalled knowing them as, laughed at her. The penis bearing villagers of power, influence or good looks gazed upon her as a deposed queen who finally was sentenced to be what a monarch fears most---becoming a commoner. Tanya's mother and his son marched up to Stefan, firing blasts of disapproval into his eyes.

"What did you do?" Stefan's wife, Svetlana, demanded to know.

"And why did you come back here?" Sasha, her son and second in command, sporting a new suit, blasted out to his father.

Stefan took in a deep breath, looked at and into his 'good wife' and more clever than wise son, letting them try to guess what he would come back with. After several volleys of anger, confusion then fear overtook their faces, and everyone else who was watching him, he pushed his outer lips into an understanding smile.

"I'm here to teach you all this!" Stefan proclaimed, as a true Commander and perhaps Comrade. He whipped out a mirror from the cart of wares, paying for the purchase of such, avoiding his usual and once beloved habit of overpaying for goods he wanted or needed. Then he confidently strode over to his daughter and gently lifted Tanya up from the ground. As he did, she spat into his face. He wiped the phlegm from his cheeks, pulled open his sash, and wiped off his distraught daughter's chin, forehead, and eyes. He cajoled and then forced his daughter to look at her reflection. "Look at it. Look!" he commanded. "Until you see that the view is not so bad," he continued in a gentle voice. A gentility based on knowledge rather than ignorance. "Or irreversible," he added. "If you, I, and everyone here have anything to say about it."

He looked at the faces of his new 'command'. They were civilians, yes, but he was in charge now. "Everyone gives according to their abilities and takes according to their needs. In the service of… us all, and not ourselves." As for what that 'us all' meant, a deeper definition found its way into Stefan's soul than I imagined possible for any man, horse, or Deity.

# CHAPTER 11

"You are what you wear," I've heard said. Stefan was still wearing his Russian Imperial Army uniform. But it lacked the two-headed eagle, which signified alliance with the Czar and the 'White Russians who opposed the Reds. His attire also did not display the Red Star, indicating affiliation with the Bolsheviks. But now, he wore his 'Russia whatever it will become' uniform with more intensity than before his ingestion of scientifica fructum afferentem. In one way, conversations with me, and two-way exchanges with people who could tolerate his being emotionally distanced from, Stefan criticized the Reds and the Whites, because neither side would consider a 'pink' government which combined the best elements of each of their ideologies. And with that same intensity, he offered 'yes, but' to everyone's optimism that Ukraine is, and now officially should be, its own country, pointing out that of Nationalist dictators in Kiev were just as corrupt as any commissar in Moscow.

"It is a basic rule of physics, shit rises to the top masquerading as Shinola. We Slavs are so used to being shit on that we prefer manure to be dumped on our heads from anyone, particularly one of 'our own', Stefan reminded Eva Lubinska over a meal of goulash and well cooked pork at the tavern. "And let us not forget that a year after we Slavs finally threw Ivan the Terrible off his throne, we invited and begged him to come back to it," he continued to the scrawny 70-year-old Polish schoolteacher across the blood-stained wooden table from him. '

Professor Lubinska's hair was white and thinning, but her bright blue eyes were still as defiant and kind as they were when she had left her hopefully soon to be recognized as a country again homeland thirty years and five failed revolutions ago.

"This is very interesting, Stafan," she replied with a calm demeanor and the slightest of affirmative nods, struggling to swallow the half-chewed hard bread soaked in soup in her nearly toothless mouth. "You refer to the people here as 'we Slavs' rather than 'native Ukrainians' or 'overstaying their welcome Russians' or…refugees like me who will have the chance to go home again after the Germans surrender in this War to End All Wars."

"Mrs. Lubinska, there is no such thing as a War to end all wars," Stefan replied to the now old woman who, when younger and with a body as beautiful as her mind was intelligent, had taught him to read and write. And, to critically think about what was said, written, and believed. With the kind of respect and camaraderie that Iankovia's 'in residence for good' schoolteacher expressed to no one else. The depth of understanding in Stefan's eyes that I observed through the window clearly indicated that he was feeling the excessive power possible with his advanced intelligence due to, perhaps, ingestion of too many scientia fructum afferentem berries for his first meal of such. And, I suspected, subsequent snacks of the fruit when he left me in the coral at home. "Humans are selfish, sadistic, and masochistic creatures who---" the Cossack Einstein continued, smoking his pipe like Old before his time Albert. "Yes, humans are self-destructive creatures who---"

"---Are created in the image of God," Mrs. Lubinska interjected', after which she blew apart the rings of putrid smoke he had set into the humid air before they found their way to the hole in the roof "Thank Christ, we are made in the image of Ultimate Effective Goodness" she continued, crossing herself in the Catholic rather than Eastern Orthodox manner. A gesture that, if done by anyone else in the Don River Tavern, would be met with a request from the management to leave the establishment. "We have to believe in the power of good if we are to eliminate evil, my dear Stefan. Even in a village where you were the only student I had who truly learned what I was trying to teach. To teach you to be kind…and, if you survive as long as I did, wise."

"Yes," Stefan considered, stroking his chin in a professorial manner under his, perhaps because of the berries he had overdosed on, or perhaps because of the rapid aging it caused, overgrown thick greying mustache, just like Captain Ivanoff's. Stefan hid his thoughts well behind his very… 'different' eyes. Finally, he concluded, then proclaimed, "But, my still highly respected Mrs

Lubinska, it's more effective to be clever than wise. Because, after all…."

He hesitated, 'felting' the thoughts and feelings going around the room and coming in from the open window. Then he stamped his boots on the floor three times, 'inviting' everyone in the tavern to have in his conversation, an invitation that no one dared refuse. "Heaven watches and earth works! Which all of us should be doing!" Stefan pontificated, with the same voice that he had used when substituting for a 'convalescing in an undisclosed location' Father Basili last Sunday at the Good (and absent) Father's pulpit. "And as for deception, laziness, or greed, or being anything except humble!" Stefan declared as an all-powerful god. "Revenge will come swiftly from events, new governments, mother nature, or…" Stefan spotted in the darkest corner of the tavern, Ilya Vladovitch, the foreman who had seen to it that the highest bidder always got all of the best goods at the river dock, at the expense of the low bidders, leaving Iankovia with empty pockets or as ghosts.

Fear now overtook Iliya's eyes, allowing entry of Stefan's words to penetrate through them to the exact place in his brain, mind, and soul my once friend and, to him anyway, now boss, aimed at.

"Ghosts will have their revenge!" Stefan declared. "Ghosts of dead soldiers, whose blood stained this table I am sitting at, and the floor where you are hiding, Iliya Vladovitch. Who is defending this country? Or civilians who died because of the oil you, and your associates, and bosses, whoever they are, sold to the enemy," Stefan blasted into the most superstitious or perhaps most open to new experiences 'mobster' in the hard working Cossack village that had turned into a pirates' den during Stefan's absence since the Great War began. Or, as Stefan now knew more and more with each recollection of rosy colored memories from his past, since before he was born.

"And remember, there is no honor amongst thieves," Father Stefan reminded the congregation. "Even less honor and more horrible consequences for those who turn in thieves for personal profit, although..." He removed envelopes from his pocket. "Special pardons are available for those who are instrumental in confessing what they have done and relating what is being done, before anyone else does. So you can have a fresh start. Just like the thief on the cross, whom Jesus forgave after said thief accepted his punishment. That thief is in Paradise as we speak, forgiven for his sins." Stefan took in a deep breath that penetrated down to his gut, then redirected his next blast of primal fire. "And as for what is the worst of all sins, yes, it is cowardice," Stefan went on, looking at and into his draft-dodging brother Andrei. "Such is redeemable with brave acts on earth, Corporal Denosevic."

With that, Stefan tossed a badge to Andrei, who accepted it with gratitude. "Yes, Sir," Stefan's older and more clever brother said with a courtly bow as he pinned it on his chest. "I will---"

"---Refrain from certain pleasures as well," Stefan said, his eyeline moving over towards his wife Svetlana.

"Despite past transgressions which resulted in events and genetics which we all have to work with now…" he continued, looking with disappointment at his son and daughter, whose noses, eyes, and chins looked more like their uncle than himself "…Together!" Stefan then declared in the manner of a Cossack Hetman. Inspiring his clan to join in a holy battle against oppression and evil. In the Cause of…well…a God that Stefan still wanted to believe in, but now had to become himself. "When we serve each other, and our fellow citizens of the world, we serve ourselves. Each gives according to their abilities, and takes according to their needs and…a modest amount of wants. Wants and needs are becoming the same thing. Right?"

After a round of 'yeses', 'so true' and 'hurrahs', initiated by Corporal Andrei, Stefan requested the musical instrument bearing patrons to begin playing, starting with the mandolin player, and two other musicians who played with too much heart to be professionally paid. Mandolin, harmonica, tambourine, and fiddle somehow found their way into becoming one sound. Chatter around the room commenced. Positive chatter, so I heard. Which Stefan was able to decipher.

Stefan was served a large bottle of brandy, "On the house, Captain Hetman Denosevic", the wife of the owner said in Ukrainian, after getting permission from her usually miserly husband. For which Stefan paid her in American greenbacks and German Deutschmarks. How he obtained them, I didn't know. And knew enough not to ask. But Mrs. Lubinska DID prepare to ask as Stefan poured a generous portion of the most expensive brew in the house into her glass.

"He, or she, who asks too many questions gets too many answers." Stefan's reply, anticipating the words about to come out of her mouth.

"What kind of answers?" she requested, after sniffing the elixor, finding it to her liking, but refraining from experiencing its aroma with her parched tongue.

"Irrelevant ones, for now," Stefan replied. "But necessary towards a commonly agreed upon destiny and solution."

"Which is what?" the woman who had been Stefan's teacher, mentor, surrogate mother, and protector pressed, gently.

"A free Poland, a free Ukraine, a free world," the reply..

"Freedom being…what, Hetman Captain Stefan?"

Stefan had to think about this one. After deep reflection, considering his advanced intelligence about the way things were and his hopefully still lingering wisdom about how they should be, he withdrew his stare from looking behind his eyes, to directing his answer in a forward direction. "Freedom is the ability to choose what Mission you are owned by, often without knowing the rules of the road you progress onto, which is called…hmmm…"

"Life," Professor (as she had been called in her homeland anyway) Lubinska replied, leading Stefan into an even more challenging forest containing foliage he had to use without identifying it. "To which we will drink!" she said to Stefan with her hoarse, baritone-like voice. Then, to me, with her still, for reasons I couldn't ascertain, hopeful eyes.

# CHAPTER 12

As the cold spring of 1918 gave way to a muddy summer, and yet another poor national harvest in the fall, desertions from the Russian Army at the front outnumbered the conscriptions. The Kaiser and the Austrian Emperor were winning more battles than they lost, at least on their Eastern Front. The Korinsky government in Petersburg and Moscow was unable to repair in a few short months the damage done to the 95 percent of Russians who possessed barely 5 percent of the wealth by Czar Nicholas III and his predecessors for three centuries.

Why history had chosen Russia, the most backward country in Europe, to be transformed into a Worker's Paradise while the countries West of her borders still rigidly held on to Capitalism, I did not know. But, as kings and kaisers know, or should know anyway, keep the masses a bit hungry and you can buy them off with bread, cake, and the occasional taste of baklava. Starve them, and they will rebel. Such was the fuel that brought the Bolsheviks into power in Russia. And as for what Russia was, that was changing as well. And who was in charge, that became a 'local' affair. As for the village, soon to be city, of

Ivankovia, Stefan retained his position as Czar, President, Philosopher King, and Comrade Commander. His ability to read minds, and sometimes hearts, resulted in few of the citizens of Ivankovia looking him in the eye when addressing their grievances. Yes, he did appear to listen to others, but did he merely hear them? He seemed to know more than he shared with me, or even Mrs. Lubinska.

Word spread rapidly about the new rules for buying oil, wheat, and non-human meat from Ivankovia at the port. Those who needed it most were at the top of the list, something Stefan rigidly enforced. And for prices they could afford to pay, that was taken into active consideration, the need for supplies taking precedence over the ability to pay for them. Local black market opportunists were quickly found out by Stefan, and they were intimidated or cajoled into doing the right thing with the kind of efficiency I seldom saw in herds of humans. As to what civilians or soldiers got oil, wheat, furs, meat, and other of Iankovia's exports, national affiliations mattered less and less as the Summer merged into an uneasy Fall.

As the ''War to end all Wars' was about to conclude its fifth and final act, a multitude of 'little wars' sprouted like toxic weeds as the revenge fest redefined international borders every week. It was not unusual for children to wake up in the morning and ask their mother 'What country do we live in now?', 'Are the new generals in charge of our town wanting us to stay or making us leave?' or 'what languages should we speak when we're in the streets so they let us stay here?' Fleeing bullets, tanks, and artillery shells was hard. Running away from the Spanish flu and famine was harder. More people in need of medical services found their way to Ivankovia than ever, drawn by rumors that there was free health care, new medicines, and miracle doctors who knew how to administer them.

Thankfully, scientifica berries didn't affect Stefan's exceptional, and now godlike, ability to put together flesh that war and disease had torn apart. The only fee Stefan demanded for making you healthy again was that you 'give according to your abilities and take according to your needs'. Payment for those with or without money started with a mandatory 2-week tour of community service duty in Ivanovia, to be continued with a two-year assignment to do the same wherever you went afterwards. And if you didn't, the 'Santa Stefan' would use his clandestine connects elsewhere to be sure that life would be both miserable and horrible. Such was made believable to incoming patients by fellow patients who had returned to Ivankovia after neglecting his advice.

To extend his Mission of saving lives so they could carry on the Vision of a world utopia, Stefan established a medical school in Iankovia, converting the town hall into a hospital for wounded soldiers, nameless deserters, and civilians in need, irrespective of the patients' religion, national affiliations, or political beliefs. Said patients were forbidden to give voice to themselves while conscious.

"But what about when they're under anesthesia?" 'Comrade Doctor Stefan's most valued medical student asked his boss as a wounded Ukrainian Socialist Nationalist damned the Bolsheviks to hell for excluding God and Jesus from their Revolution while fighting to repel the ether mask over his enlarged, recently broken nose. "And what happens if this rabid dog bites me with whatever teeth he still has?" the student grunted through a forced whisper while trying to use his 150-pound body to restrain the 250-pound bear on the still-absentee former mayor's oversized desk, now converted into an operating table.

"You don't bite him back, like you did the last patient, WE saved, Sasha," Stefan whispered to his son, while assisting him in restraining the abruptly reluctant patient.

"Which YOU saved, when…." Sasha replied to his father, after which he got a glimpse of the patient's intestines spewing out of his abdomen. The 17-going-on-7 lad then spilled his own guts out on the floor.

"Doctor Sasha, here is fully qualified to save your leg and what is left of your left arm," Stefan assured the patient, taking over holding the mask covering his mouth and nose. "He has a stomach bug, is all." Stefan tried to assure the patient under his struggling arms, which were one more push away from being thrown out of their sockets.

"All you doctors are liars!" came through bouts of blood covering the overgrown beard of the passion-driven person who had become a patient, yet again, due to an escalated political dispute at the dock with a still Czar supporting (now called 'White Russian') blacksmith. "I want a real doctor!"

"Which I am," Stefan assured him, somehow finding a way to use his 160-pound exhausted body to keep the nearly 300-pound bear on his back. "And with my best doctor," he continued, motioning with his chin and penetrating eyes for Sasha to get his ass off the floor, and opinion of himself out of the dumpster, and take the thankfully unbroken bottle of ether and mask into his shaking hand. "And best nurse, Tanya!" Stefan yelled out, summoning his daughter clad in blood-soaked 'commoner' smock, her long, blonde hair neatly tucked into a scarf. He directed her to gently take hold of the angry, maybe Red or maybe White officer's hand.

A smile came to the patient's face as he looked into Tanya's eyes, his own vision blurred. "Mother?" he said.

"Yes, indeed," Stefan assured the exhausted soldier who most probably was on the run as a deserter from three different armies, having seen too many men on the battlefield see their most beloved women when they were deciding to live or die. "Mother, who wants and needs you to relax, trust her," Comrade Doctor Stefan added regarding Tanya, playing the role her father had assigned to her, with an unexpected sincerity. "And Sasha." Stefan continued, cranking his head towards his son.

Yes, Sasha, his son, who would earn his way to becoming a doctor with all the prestige that goes with it, rather than buy and fake his way into that, for the right reasons, a position of social stature in any political system.

Tanya sang to the ex-soldier, looking for the right army to voluntarily join, while Sasha used the ether to send him into, hopefully, a blissful dream state.

"And now?" Sasha asked his father. "Are you going to save him?"

"WE are going to save him," Stefan asserted to his son. He instructed Mrs. (now head nurse) Lubinska to wheel in a tray of medical supplies to the table. They included scalpels, 20th and 18th century instruments soaked in grain alcohol, herbs, modern cleansing equipment, and something from the modern world that seemed odd to most of even the most highly educated surgeons. Surgical gloves, which were purchased with either the sale of petrol or by threatening the well-being of a well-fed crewmanning an overstocked boat en route to an aristocrat's estate, or a general's private quarters. Neither I nor Mrs. Lubinska got a straight answer when we asked questions regarding such.

"Are you sure he's going to make it?" Sasha asked his father as the latter made him wash his hands in the newly installed sink, then glove up..

"Yes," Tanya said, while prepping the patient's belly and arm, her recently blistered fingers shaking while doing such. "You make all of these guarantees to everyone.and---"

"---So far, have delivered on," Stefan interjected, taking a scalpel in hand. He forced his eyes into a maximally wide position, letting in everything they could send to his brain so that all of the 'data' could connect in ways that only the intuitive soul can understand, or implement. "I promise that all that I say we can do, we will do. Including saving this man's life, even though God and Mother Nature say it's our place to let him go to his final resting place."

"But how?" Sasha demanded to know. "Just a few months ago, and before you left for the War, you were so, you know---,"

"---Happy?" Stefan replied. He let out a reflective sigh, then focused those oculars on the patient's flesh, and his own, for better or worse, 'brilliant in the ways of the world' soul. "Yes, I know…Now more than ever," the hyper-intelligent cynic added as he dared fate again. Knowing that the patient's condition was worse than good. As was the world around him. But still, somehow, believing that one could make it good again. As long as you understood enough about the bad."

# CHAPTER 13

The grass behind Stefan's house was less green and more scrawny than in the pastures owned by everyone else, but he insisted on my being there. "Because if you get too rich in the belly, you get poorer between the ears," he told me. But both of us knew that it was the best way to see that no one would take revenge on him by doing harm to or stealing me. And, he needed to have some company after a long day of creating an independent, honorable, and sustainable Camelot, its borders extending beyond the village borders under the noses of larger countries which had been established before the Great War. And those that were emerging as the War was coming to an end.

Inside the shack that had been converted to a house in her legal husband's absence, Svetlana read the newspaper in her bedroom. "So," I heard her say to Stefan as he strode into the room, taking off his boots, caked with a new layer of frozen late November muck.. "The Bolsheviks have officially taken over the Russian government, declaring that Russia is no more at War with Germany, giving to the Kaiser a third of European Russian land."

"Which doesn't include the People's Democratic Kingdom of Ivankovia!" Stefan declared, with kingly pride, slipping out of his frost-covered coat.

"And the Reds, as they now like to be called, have given away a third of the Russian and Ukrainian speaking people in Euro-Russia," she noted. "Which we still are."

"And will remain so," he assured her in Ukrainian and Russian, removing his tunic.

"And that Comrade Lenin will be restructuring the Army and the new Soviet society, placing Good Communists on top. And selfish Capitalists on the bottom, along with Cossacks who lament the abdication of the still living Czars," she continued. "With power now being centralized in Moscow, where you have not been."

"In body, yes," Stefan replied, glancing in the mirror, combing the loose hairs on his enlarged Stalinesque mustache with a trace of Lenin's goatee under it.

"So," Svetlana said, playing down the newspaper. "How is it that you still wield as much power with judges, politicians, and generals in Moscow now as you did when the aristocratic Czar was in charge, then the Moderate Socialist Mensheviks, and then, as you and they say, due to justice serving necessity, radical Revolutionary Bolsheviks?"

Stefan looked to me as to how to answer his still, for reasons I didn't understand, his beloved wife's question. A wife with whom he used to share all of his secrets. He now related less of his thoughts, feelings, and plans to.

"You know, or should know, Stefan," Svetlana interjected to break the 'more not said than said' conversation going on between me and the pathologically idealist Cossack I had converted into a cynic who kept more secrets than I, or Mrs Libniska, did. "For everything you say to me, there are ten things you don't, my dear Stefan."

"Just returning the favor, my, for reasons I don't understand, more dear Svetlana," Stefan said to her reflection in the mirror. "And, as there are favors we can do for each other, and the world, perhaps we should get to…hmmm…business," he stated, after which he unbuttoned his trousers, taking them off, then faced his wife, naked. "Now you, please," he asked, gently.

"And if I don't strip down and let you have your way with me, you'll use your connections with Comrade Lenin to have me sent to a Gulag, like, so it is said anyway, you did with other 'criminals to the People's Revolution'?" she barked back.

"People say things that sometimes aren't true," he assured her. "But, it could be true, out of necessity."

"The necessity for you to be king of this 'people's paradise' you say you are building here?" she challenged.

"Yes, to the motive, but not the office," his reply. "Since those who want to be king, president, or prime minister shouldn't be trusted with the job," he mused. "And, as for my position here, I'm just as the Capitalistic Americans, who are about to abolish the Socialist experiment as part of an Imperialist expeditionary force, would say…a temp."

Svetlana pretended to laugh.

"I'm only here now to see who was and still is the boss of a crooked, dishonest, and people-harming 'mafia' that took over our town, our lives, and your soul," he explained. "And see that he, or she, will be… inactivated. Or, if possible, converted to a Higher Cause."

"And fucking me you'll be doing that job?" Svetlana shot back, folding her still clothes bearing arms.

"In the long run, maybe," Stefan replied. "Since….I would like to leave this planet with children of my own. Whose genetics combine the best elements from you, Sventlana, and me and…"

"---That horse you keep talking to like he's your lover, wife, mistress, and mentor!" Svetlana barked back.

"He's something else," Stefan reply.

"Or 'Professor' Lubinska, whose reproductive system, which---"

"---Was underused when she was young, and is now non-functional now that she is old," Stefan interjected, with regret. "But, as for us…"

"Yes, we did love each other once, a long time ago," Svetlana's reply,

"And still can, and have to, please," his reply, delivered with desperation and passion.

What Stefan said to Sventlana with his mouth or eyes after that, I didn't know. All I saw was the curtains on the windows being closed by Sventlana, affording me only a view of their silhouettes. Her exposed breasts edged their way to Stefan's chest. Their lips merged into something…special, that I thought was gone from Stefan's emotional vocabulary. Or maybe he had found a way to trick less intelligent humans like Svetlana. Or 'dumb' animals like me.

# CHAPTER 14

I've heard it said that just because everyone is out to get you, that is no reason to be paranoid. And there was no shortage of "Cossack Comrades' in Iankovia who wanted to 'get' Stefan. Most particularly, his brother, Andrei. Who, Captain Stefan, who had now taken to wearing Cossack warrior attire fashioned after the uniform of 17<sup>th</sup> century rebel Taras Bulba, had conscripted as a deputy corporal in his 'ARMY'. An Army which, in reality, numbered one masochist officer in search of masochistic Truth. And a conscript who passed along lies and a few truths from his now-smarter brother, more interested in the money he got for delivering envelopes to people of power and influence outside of Iankovia than their contents, which he was unable to read anyway, given that he was dyslexic.

"So, who are we going to side with, Comrade Stefan?" Andrei, clad in more contemporary 'assimilated Cossack' civilian attire, asked his brother from atop his favorite horse, Natasha, while perusing the lowlands below the highest point in Iankovia. "The Reds from Moscow who want to invite us into their 'give according to your ability and take according to their needs' Socialist Experiment," he said, looking to the clouds gathering under the Northern sky. "The Whites and their supporters from the West who want to welcome us into their 'free market' world where anyone can get as rich as he, or she, can," he noted glancing to the sun setting over the Steppes, conferring a golden hue over the horizon and the abundant fields of wheat and still pumping oil rigs. "Then there are the Blacks, as they call themselves," he continued, looking to the West. "Anarchists who say that Democratic Socialism should have no rules, but each of their commanders will slit your throat if anyone violates or criticizes their 'suggested ways' to manage a village, city or town, or country." Looking further Westward, he continued, "Then there is the 'Expeditionary forces'. The 'good guys' in the War against the 'evil' Axis powers of Germany, Austria, and Turkey. American, British, French, Czech, Greek, and even some Japanese soldiers who are being informed that they have to neutralize the Reds and colonize Russia as well as Poland into 'free states' who will serve the Capitalists in Washington, London, Paris, Athens, and Tokyo. Or," he went on, looking southward, "The Ukrainian nationalists who see us as the petrol station and breadbasket of THEIR new country, with its capital in Kiev. Which has changed hands six times in as many months, and no doubt will have six changes of flags flying over its Parliament Building before all of this is over. But..." he continued, looking at and, to the extent he could, into Stafan's hyperactive brain through his now very open eyes. "You know that."

"Yes, I do," Stefan said, wishing he was still a naive Christian, Democratic, Socialist, Nationalist,

Internationalist, Anarchist, and, if the dead Czars could be replaced, Benign Monarchist. ..

"So," Andrei inquired of his brother as the latter nearly lost himself in reminiscent reflection. "What are you, or rather, 'we', trying to establish here?"

Stefan took in a deep breath, lamenting, as I did, the 'you have to go with ONE ideological option at the exclusion of all the others' situation going on everywhere else in what used to be the Russian Empire. After coming to yet another conclusion, he kept to himself, and he allowed his pursed lips to merge into a smile. One that was kind and gentle, yet firm in its compassionate convictions. "What we are trying to build here is a democratic, Spiritual rather than Orthodox Christian Cossack village that combines the most effective and kindest elements of all ideologies," he said, looking at his brother, while stroking my neck, as he knew I did have eyes that could see everything behind my head. "Which will bring back the traditional Cossack life to all Ukrainians, and Russians, if they want to come here.. And even Tatar Turks or Catholic Poles. And even, as we used to call them, 'Christ Killer' Jews. Who would not have to convert to being Orthodox Christians to stay here, establish their own businesses here, or marry one of ours."

"Including your daughter?" Andrei challenged. "While you give an interfaith sermon from the altar of your church, quoting the Koran, Torah, Bible, and Das Kapital? And the US Constitution, which guarantees the right to the pursuit of happiness AND separation of Church and state?"

Stefan reflected on the challenge. Impressed that his anti-literate brother had actually learned how to read, or was being read to by someone other than himself. Maybe Mrs Lubinska. Or his (theoretically anyway) ex-mistress, Svetlana. Or someone else. Perhaps the real 'boss' of the Ivankovian mafia, who was secretly waiting to retake Stefan's place as 'king' in a village that, in reality, had never had a fairly and freely elected leader, since the (theoretically, anyway) 'golden' Cossack days a hundred years ago.

"So, who do we sell our oil, wheat, livestock, horses, and, if it comes to it, young boys who want to become soldiers to?" Andrei inquired. "The Whites, the Reds, the Anarchists, the Ukrainian Nationalists, or the even better armed victorious Expeditionary Forces who will soon discover that the stories about there being contagious plague, quicksand, boat swallowing undercurrents in the river and poisonous plants around this 'kingdom' of, as you say' 'ours', are as false as the ability of that horse of yours to talk with you in 'human speak'?

"We are untouched by the outside world as long as you keep spreading my messages to the people of power and influence," the Philosopher King of the newly established country of Utopia said to Andrei.

"And how are we going to get what we really need when what we have runs out? With food we can't grow, machines we can't build, and books that you say we should all read?" is the next challenge to Stefan's agenda.

'By you delivering my messages to those in need," Stefan said. "Or those who are smart enough to NOT be nationalists, or any other kind of 'ist'. Those who have universal compassion for all in need, and not just for family, friends, and fellow countrymen. And who will hold fair elections where whoever counts the votes does not want or need to be in power," the reply, delivered into Andrei's angry face.

Andrei's grimace turned into a smile, one that ridiculed Stefan's idealistic beliefs and firmly held convictions. "You know," Andrei said with a surrogate paternal tone after a chuckle, which his 'younger and formerly dumber' brother ignored. "God protects fools. You are not a fool anymore," he said with a congratulatory tone, which abruptly turned into a challenging one. "And every time you go off to 'the wilderness to hear the voice of God without the chatter of his most frustrating and beloved creation,' you come back more… distanced from the rest of us."

"Yes, I know," Stefan said, his head turned downward, with a sorrowful tone.

"The Lord above, for reasons I still don't understand, also protects drunks," Andrei said with breath reeking of vodka, offering his brother a swig from his canteen, which was supposed to be filled with water.

"Yes, I remember being told that by our father, who lived longer than he deserved to," Stefan replied as he refused the elixir that would make his brain stop thinking so fast and intensely, giving his soul a much-desired rest.

"But as for you, and maybe all of us, God is doing more watching than doing these days, I will take his place and protect you," Corporal Andrei said, placing his bear-like paws on Stefans' shaking shoulders. "If that is alright with you, Comrade Captain."

"Yes, of course, Lieutenant Andrei," Stefan said to his brother. After which he pinned on his hand-made non-White and non-Red Russian Army tunic one of the medals given to him by Captain Ivanov. Stefan gave his brother a brisk salute, which was returned in kind.

"And, the next set of messages to deliver to the outside world, with a map as to where the recipient might be," Stefan said, giving his brother an envelope. "And..." he continued, taking a small vial of powder from his pocket, handing it to his brother.

"Someone who, perhaps, gave you this medal?" Andrei's reply.

I wondered how and why Andrei 'guessed' that it was inevitable for Captain Ivanov, and his former comrades in his Platoon from the Great War, to get access to the cloistered and resource-rich village-kingdom of Iankovia. But Stefan was sure that the answer was not something that I needed to know, especially because I wanted to know.

"You know," Stefan said, placing his hand on Andrei's shaking shoulder. "There is a reason why I asked you to contact the representatives from the Blacks, Reds, Whites, Nationalists, and Expeditionaries who were my comrades in the Great War. Who, according to your information, are fighting each other now, right?"

"A strange coincidence, yes, but such is true," Andrie said to his brother, truthfully this time.

"And that you," Stefan replied, staring at and into the terrified sibling master who he now owned, "my once cruel but not by necessity kind brother, guide them, and only them, to find their way here. Blindfolded."

"So you can open their eyes?" Andrei inquired.

"Or shoot a bullet into them, if necessary. If what I, and only I, see is what is behind them, because they are, now anyway…" Stefan replied.

"Useful idiots?" Andrei inquired. "Like you used to be?"

"And am not anymore, thank you, well…" Stefan said, removing his hand from Andre's shoulder, raising it up to the sky. "Whatever might be up there," he continued. "Or, in here," he added, placing his hand on his heart. "Or here," he went on, tapping Andrei's chest.

With that, Stefan trotted me down to the village square over dirt roads that finally were covered with easily breakable melting ice, while Lieutenant Andrei galloped his horse North by Northwest through the sufficiently but not excessively snow-covered grasslands.

The sun finally set, darkness coming over the Steppes faster than normal. The moon was determined to shine its way through the clouds over it. Which it did, thankfully for those under it. Some of those are under it anyway.

# CHAPTER 15

Order One, issued by the Petrograd Issue of Soviet Workers and Soldiers with the boldest of signatures back in March 1917, did more than disallow officers to punish enlisted men if they didn't address them as 'Your Excellency'. It opened the door for every man and woman, in uniform or standardized working attire, to think for themselves, or be free to have their thinking changed by propaganda from officers and bosses other than those of the Czar's Imperial Army or the Czar. But when the last of the Romanov Dynasty abdicated, there was no common enemy for everyone in Russia to hate, fear, or worship. It was now about ideologies based on what was written in books to be adopted by 'liberated' populations who, to an underestimated extent, didn't know how to read. In a war between at least four different sides that allowed NO one to be neutral. Anyone who dared to incorporate the best elements of different ideologies would be misunderstood, marginalized, or shot.

Stefan, clad as an 18th-century warrior Cossack doing summer haying, carried an extra bail of hay into the coral outside the tavern, which was officially closed to all but his specially invited guests for a post-Christmas gathering. "It's a bit much, I know," he said to me as the weight of the square bail clogged whatever musicality in his voice still remained after his Scientifica-induced opening of the brain tissue that allowed him to see the dirt in people rather than the false rosy colored exterior. "But you aren't going to be the only horse in this corral soon," he continued after dumping the bale in front of my feet, then shaking his now foot-long warlock in the middle of his freshly shaved head. "Andrei, who for reasons of practicality, is not allowed to sport a Cossack warlock because he has to seem to be an equal to non-Cossacks outside of our small and growing kingdom, will soon be bringing in the men who called me a hard-working Comrade but who considered me an entertaining and medically necessary fool. And as is so often the case, you are what you ride. Therefore, I apologize for the kind of equine company you'll have to keep when Andrei brings them here. I'll leave the window open so I can hear any problems you have with them. But, at least they are company. And for a horse, bad or boring company is better than no company, right?"

"I snorted a 'no, not in my case anyway,' to Stefan. He misinterpreted it as a 'yes' Despite becoming increasingly alone with every rise in IQ points, he grew in his rapidly developing brain. Since he had taken it upon himself to make his home village of Iankovia a model independent state that would eventually spread its Enlightenment to every other region of the now disintegrating Imperial Russian Empire, he was misinterpreting much of what I was trying to say to him and show him. However, there was one thing he still understood: the ideal feed for the body, mind, and spirit of any country was a mixture of Bolshevik corn, Christian Socialist molasses, White Russian barley, Anarchist oats, and a generous proportion of Ukrainian Internationalism bran.

When indulging in a generous portion of such from the grain barrel he gave to me, a gentle flow of snowflakes fell from the grey sky. I wondered if the horses I would 'be in charge of would have the same kind of connection with their riders that I had with Stefan. As for that Connection, we were still Comrades in a very (to the world, anyway) uncommon Cause, with, for the moment, enough common goals to keep us going, but with different strategies on how to obtain those lofty yet globally necessary goals.

"I know," Stefan said to me as he patted me on the newly grown winter coat on my neck, regarding what I was thinking and feeling. An idealistic smile suddenly appeared on his face, the kind he had before I turned him into an altruistic and intelligence-burdened cynic. "It's just you and me now, not against, but FOR the world!" he declared. "Starting with…" he pointed towards the first dinner guest emerging on horseback through a well-wooded trail to the North of us. A blindfolded mounted Colonel wearing an Imperial Russian Army uniform with white bandages over the sleeves and several decals showing the double eagle coat of arms championing the Czar and his divine Right to rule, complemented by an Eastern Orthodox crucifix around his neck. A garment he wore with pride, perhaps because of its affiliation, or the medals pinned to his chest, which blinded my eyes when the sun decided to penetrate its rays through the clouds.

"You can take your blindfold off, Captain Ivanov, which I know you tried to take off before, despite your pledge not to," Stefan yelled out to the Colonel in a friendly tone to his former boss, superior, and, sometimes anyway, protector. "And, as promised," he continued as he pulled out a large leather pouch from under his sash. "The gold, jewels, and coins my brother promised you are yours to keep for yourself or share with your new superiors."

"Which I will," Ivanov said as he removed the blindfold. "Hand to God, Lieutenant Denosevic," he said, raising his right hand in a pledge, his left angrily pulling away the reins of his horse away from Andrei's grip.

"It's HETMAN Denosevic!" Stefan exclaimed, with no shortage of pride or dedication, for the first time adopting the title of his revered Cossack ancestors. "Welcome to the free and international state of Iankovia, which I regret to inform you was not named after you, Nicholi Iankovia," he continued, after which he threw the overloaded purse to the promoted officer in the White Army.

Though the throw was catchable by any half blind boy, Ivanov's thinly gloved hand could not hold onto the purse. Seeing the riches in jewels, nuggets, and coin spread over the snow-covered ground, Ivanov dismounted with a firm action of his right leg, then a painful extraction of his left from the stirrup, his horse seeing the opportunity to escape from its rider. On his aching knees, the aristocratic born White Army Colonel who refused to bend down to pick up a kopek that had fallen to the floor when at headquarters or a chunk of stew meat that had dropped to the ground when at the front in (what would certainly be called) First World War desperately gathered the contents of the reward for coming for re-union dinner like a man who had not eaten anything other than weeds and leaves for weeks. And by the fresh wounds on arms, and way his tunic hung loose over his thin waist, he had indeed finally paid the price for his promotion and military honors. Was he always cool and collected, an aristocrat, in such a state from having fought Bolsheviks who stole from, acquired, and burnt down the estates he had boasted about? Were his wounds incurred from fighting against the 'godless communists' who were burning down and looting churches his family had worshipped in and contributed to? Such was immaterial. It was no surprise that Ivanov had sided with the Whites when the Red Army declared itself the guardian of what had been the Imperial Russian Empire.

"So, what are we going to do with him?" I thought, and Stefan gave voice to, at the same time, regarding the militarily inept Imperial Army Captain who had risen up the ranks in the White Army to nearly the position of General so quickly, for reasons which, for now, were irrelevant. "I'm offering you a post as a General in the Army of the Republic of Ivankovia, 'Comrade Colonel," Stefan said with a confident grin and upturned chin, having put an angry grimace on Ivanov's for the first time in Stefan's memory, stubble-covered face. "A joke, Your Excellency' Hetman Stefan continued with a courtly bow.

"Will I get another bag of these?" Ivanov asked, regarding the wealth in his pocket, which he might take back for his fellow Whites or keep for himself, now that most Armies were paid more in loot than the monetary pay promised by their idealistic commanders. As for monetary currency, with the exception of American dollars or British Pounds, such was becoming more worthless each day due to runaway and intentionally created inflation. However, there was another form of currency, besides food, that was becoming increasingly valuable each day. "And if I decide to join this Iankovian Army of yours," Ivanov pressed. "Will I get a horse who knows that his place is between my legs and not three feet away from me whenever I try to catch him?" he continued as he futilely tried to catch the black mare he rode in on. An overworked, in-season Morgan with granulated wounds on her left hip and right neck, who seemed to be more interested in me than any conversation between her 'master. '

I didn't have the heart to tell the mare that my breeding days were over, voluntarily. I'd find out later what she heard, or understood, from her most recent master about the War going on outside of Ivankovia, which had taken the lives of so many people, and horses.

"Private, I mean, Hetman Stefan," Ivanov begged of my 'master' after four failed tries to grab the black mare's reins, the fifth landing Ivanov's ass then face in the mud and manure-soaked snow in the corral. "How did you find me? And why did you find me!?" he demanded. "And tell me a few magic words that can make this horse listen to me, please."

"I will," Stefan said, with more arrogance than pride. "But first you have to reach an agreement," he continued. "With him."

"YOUR horse? Achilles?" Ivanov asked.

"No, him!" the new Hetman said, pointing the decorated White Army Colonel to a plainly clad blindfolded ride of the same rank in a uniform identical to his, with the exception of the lack of epilates on the shoulder, medals on the chest and double eagle insignia, on his cap, the latter replaced by a Red Star.

With quick reflexes, fueled by alacrity you could see and fear you could smell, Ivanov pulled out his revolver, pointing it at the next blindfolded guest Andrei escorted in from another holding area beyond a cluster of snow-covered pine trees. Ivanov's use of his weapon was halted by a slap of Stefan's fist on his former commander's wrist. Ivanov's weaponless hand turned into a clenched fist.

"Any thoughts of using that pistol or any other weapon against Achilles, and the next slap will be done with this, Comrade Excellency Sir!" Stefan barked out, whipping out his sabre.

"Fine," Ivanov blurted out as the blindfolded Red Army officer's horse was led into another corral. "But his Bolshevik Devils burnt down my estate. And took into custody any servant who wouldn't join their Army. An estate which my father built with his own hands from the ground up!"

"Hands that had no blisters on them, while supervising servants who did the work!" the rider screamed as he was guided in towards the tavern, then helped off his horse. "And those servants are being re-educated to serve themselves and the Collective rather than an aristocratic class of bourgeois capitalists who owned 95 percent of the wealth and land! Aristocrats who, when asked if they could share just half of what they stole from the people, said they wouldn't! And when you Whites came to MY village to try to own it and its people again, at the point of a gun, and to burn it to the ground if we didn't tell you where the Christian Socialists were, we----"

"Sergeant Boyco?" Ivanov gasped, finally recalling where he had heard the voice before.

"Comrade Colonel Boyco," the former Sergeant under Ivanov's command boasted, allowing Andrei the honor of pulling off his blindfold. "Who didn't have to take off this blindfold to see where we were heading?"

"Because you could see through it?" Ivanov grunted. "And because well…maybe you were promised a private reward if you came here alone," he continued as Boyco was given his 'post Christmas dinner' giftbag. Upon seeing it, Boyco's eyes opened wider than any time he had 'stumbled' onto booty in the Great War as a supply Sergeant who kept a generous 'finder's fees' for himself before sharing it with the men he was charged to keep fed, clothed, and sheltered. "I'm sure being a man of wealth now, you'll share it with the Collective."

"Yes, he will," Stefan interjected.

"No, he won't," Ivanov shot back. "The Marxist Credo that even you, Hetman Denosevic, kept saying is 'each gives according to his abilities and takes according to their needs'. An ideal that doesn't take place outside of the library. The person who works harder and smarter deserves to have more than the person who is lazy or stupid."

"Stupid according to your definition of it, still 'Captain' Ivanov?" Boyco shot back.'You keep the working men tired, overworked, and illiterate by denying them the time, money, and dignity to read or think for themselves. And when they start to think for themselves, because of finally getting fed up with being underfed, and seeing their children starve, while yours dine on gourmet meals we cook, we prepare, and we clean up afterward, those working men, and women---"

"Destroy everything Holy and Righteous!" Ivanov screamed out. "Like this!" he continued, grabbing hold of the crucifix around his neck.

"Jesus was a Communist!" Boyco pointed out.

"Said by a godless Communist who wants to ban all religion."

"Because religion as it is practiced now by the rich priests is toxic! The poor are supposed to suffer here on earth, while you rich are allowed to enslave and steal from them, so that the poor and enslaved will get their reward in Heaven?" Boyco blasted out. He took in a deep breath, then fired out another round. "YOUR Jesus said that it's easier for a camel to go through the eye of a needle than for a rich man to get into Heaven. Unless, of course, that rich man gives a small 'gift' to the Church in exchange for the priest giving him a special ticket to enter Paradise, while that rich man continues to steal from anyone he can. Because he is a caring man, of course, caring for the needs and wants of his own family at the expense of everyone else's!" No....what we need is universal compassion for everyone. That everyone is the collective. Which is served by---"

"----Freedom," came from a voice of another blindfolded rider escorted to another corner of the corral. "Freedom from oppression from EVERYONE. Freedom from ALL government and rule made by government. Including Bolshevicks, Socialists, and Libertarians who think we need a rule book to rule ourselves fairly and compassionately."

"Vlodmir Melmyk!" Boyco and Ivanov blurted out of the dropped jaws in unison upon seeing the third guided rider taking off his blindfold.

"Anarchy is the only solution, with ALL men, and women being free to do and say what they want," Melmyk said as he leaped off his horse, every stitch of his clothing, including his medal free leather coat, pitch black. "I suggested to a Red Army 'morale' officer that even though religion is the opiod of the masses, everyone has the right to privately overdose on the toxin of their choice, as a suggestion cloaked as a joke. Which got me this!" he said of a fresh red scar on his forehead. "And when I went behind the back of the new White Russian Mayor after his goons took over my village, to give the food they stole from the Reds to the people who are starving most first, I got this," he continued, laying his finger on and into a slash on his cheek which extended into his mouth. "After which he said that the Russian Empire can only be restored to its former greatness, which in reality was anything but great by---"

"---Foreign intervention," came from another escorted rider and dinner guest, in a refined businessman's accent. He was dressed in a three-piece tweed European suit with a tie, much like the one I saw in pictures of Vladimir Lenin when he was giving speeches to workers clad in factory overalls. "From foreign investors and benefactors, who some say are invading our country but who we need to save it from itself," he continued, pointing miniature flags of the US, Great Britain, France, and Japan on his lapel. The crown of his head was bald as a lemon, reflecting the sunlight that shone upon it with a painful to look at glare, much like Lenin's. But when his larger-than-life full-faced blindfold was taken off, there was no moustache and goatee under it—only the fair, unwrinkled skin of a man no more than thirty years old.

"Corporal Olek Koval?" Ivanov blurted out.

"Who finally lost all of his hair?" Boyco added, with a chuckle.

"And the brains under it," Melmyk added with a laugh.

"You really think that the Americans, Brits, French, Japanese, and 'we established democracy first' Greeks are invading our country to save us from the Red Terror so they can establish Free Market Capitalism that serves US? Whatever they set up will serve THEM, not us. And we'll become chopped up into colonies of their countries like China was. Fifty years ago, baldy?"

"My people can fix this!" Koval protested. He pointed to his head after gaining control of his feet on the mud, snow, and manure-covered ground with his newly shined Italian leather shoes. "And as for my hair, no grass grows on busy streets."

"That can use some overpasses," came from another rider. "I can loan you one of these," Dimitri Sokolov said, pointing to a collection of scalps on a necklace he pulled out from under his shirt once he was relieved of his horse and blindfold. This time by Sasha, Stefan's son. Whose authentic Cossack clothing was starting to fit his eyes. "Scalps from, well, all of you deluded idealists," Sokolov continued. "Which keeps me warm in winter. Taken from dead people only, since I DO have a moral code."

"That you can take whatever you want from anyone else, Dmitiri?" Melmyk barked into the exchange of ideals and ideas.

"Which you are free to do also," Sokolov, the former collector of ears, eyes, and other body parts from Austrian soldiers during the last War to end all wars, pointed out. "Including, citizen Melmyk, you taking over the leadership of the Anarchist Movement, which, on paper, says there should be no leaders. But in reality is---"

"---Part but not all of the solution we all will come up with, and implement, here and everywhere else," Stefan offered, and affirmed. "And, 'gentlemen', are you part of the solution, or do you want to continue to be part of the problem?"

Something in what Stefan said, or didn't say, resonated with his guests, all of whom were given purses of equal size and content as a 'thank you' for coming. They looked at each other, then into each other's eyes. Somehow, they found again the people they were when they were fighting in the Great War against a common enemy. For a common Cause---survival. Men who had saved each other's lives for a reason that had nothing to do with the ideologies they had now pledged exclusive loyalty to.

"Now then," Stefan said. "The pouches you have been given are yours to keep, and share. The only thing I ask of you is to share a meal with me."

"And if we're not hungry?" Ivanov, emaciated from grief as well as hardship, proposed.

"Or we have other places to liberate, conquer, or loot?" Boyco added.

"Then, hmmm," Stefan said, putting his hand over his mouth, averting his eyes. He whistled. Behind each of the visitors stood ten armed Iankovians. Some clad as

Cossacks, some as 'assimilated' Ukrainian villagers. All armed with guns, bows, swords, and determined eyes.

"You're bluffing, still, Private Denosevic," Boyco sneered at Stefan, representing the group's mutually arrived at opinion on the matter.

"Maybe I am, or maybe I'm not, but maybe you can ask them," Stefan said, as his daughter Tanya pulled in a light cart upon which was a pot of freshly prepared stew with five plates and bowls. She offered a taste of it to Boyco, ensuring that his bowl contained a generous portion of meat.

"Ask him or them if I'm bluffing," Stefan calmly related, pointing to the pieces of meat in the stew.

Boyco didn't have to taste the meat to determine it was of human origin. He allowed himself to be guided into the private dining hall by Stefan's wife, Svetlana. The rest of the politically mixed congregation followed, the door closing behind them.

I didn't know how Stefan had made chicken meal smell like human meatballs. Perhaps the stew meat was actually chicken. I didn't know what he was prepared to do for, with, or to his dinner 'guests'. But, as in all marriages, friendships, or mortal-Deity relationships, each party had their secrets. Some of which, dangerously, they didn't know they had. Maybe one of the other now riderless horses in the coral would give me a clue. Or, maybe not.

i

# CHAPTER 16

As promised, Stefan left the window open to the main room of the tavern, which had been converted into a royal dining hall, providing the attendants with a chance to indulge in authentic, deluxe Cossack cuisine, along with no shortage of other dishes that represented the best culinary accomplishments of no less than six Western European countries. He left the curtains open so I could see everything as well. Every one of the special guests was relieved of every weapon they came in with, except their mouths. The most effective instrument to secure peace or implement war for humans, as I recall lifetimes in that, theoretically anyway, most perfect of biological bodies.

The most intelligent people discuss ideas and ideals, while those with lesser intellectual development rant about events (politics and sports). Those with the least mental abilities or moral fiber chatter about who did what to whom and what they were wearing at the time.

Though Stefan tried to keep the conversation focused on ideals and ideas, it got perverted into rigid political ideologies. Then downgraded into a plethora of 'who did what to whom' reasons for Stefan's old Army 'buddies' to have chosen different sides in what was now a Civil War, with each side fighting for superiority as to whose political experiment would be tested first. As for what they were wearing at the time, that was the determining factor as to why each of the five comrades who kept each other alive during the (as it was now being named) Great War were honor and contract-bound to convert, subjugate, or kill each other. If a platoon of Whites burnt down your farm, you enlisted into the first Company of Red Soldiers that came your way while carting away your remaining belongings. If the Reds killed your son, you joined the Whites. If the Whites and the Reds imprisoned you, you became an Anarchist or Ukrainian Nationalists. If you were too Christian for the Reds, you joined the Expeditionary forces from other countries who wanted to colonize the Russian Empire. If you lost faith in God and all of the well-intended but badly executed Political Causes, the Party of your choice was you. The only mandate was to steal from whoever you could without getting caught, and to kill or be killed, no matter who entered your domain. Most tragically, and most often, if an army decided to conscript you into its ranks, even though your ideology and former affiliation were not theirs, it was an offer you couldn't refuse. But the terms of the deal were that if you deserted, the reward for such bravery, or common sense, was a bullet to the back or a noose around your neck. Or worse, those 'gifts' being bestowed on members of your family.

The idea of combining political ideologies and applying them on a case-by-case basis made sense to me, as well as Stefan. How to make that happen….well, that was the beginning of the difference between us, that creative Civil War of wits and wills between us, and within each of us.. And it started with Stefan closing the windows to the tavern, as well as the curtains. Leaving me in charge of the dinner guests' horses. And all of the belongings on them.

# CHAPTER 17

As far as I could tell, the other horses in the corral were more interested in food than conversation. In the language of my present body, I asked them where they came from and what they thought of their human masters, but got nothing back. They seemed to be conversing with each other in another language. One that I might be able to understand if I were smarter. Just as you feed your empty belly with hay, when your mind is in need of more abilities to understand itself and the minds of others, you acquire more Scientifica.

The fence around the corral was tall enough to keep even an 18-hand Thoroughbred within its perimeter. And solid enough so that a donkey would have to develop the ability to dig a tunnel to get out. However, there was one thing that the humans who spoke only the languages of their own species hadn't figured on. The ability of a horse to use its mouth to grab hold of a latch to open the gate. When it was my turn to 'stay awake' and stand guard for my assigned herd against wolves or pesky humans, it was around midnight. I used the opportunity to open the gate. It took far less effort than I thought was necessary. Noting that my equine companions had their feet locked into slumbering positions, or were lying on the soft ground after filling their bellies with hay, I snuck out and made my way to the Scientifica pasture, closing the gate behind me. Past drunken people, and slumbering animals under the light of a moon that showed me the way for ten strides, then hid behind the clouds, requiring me to smell the path forward for the next 30. Eventually, after circling only three times, I found the oil-rich pasture and electrified ground where Scientifica grew. Not sure if it was north of where I had left, or south, east, or west of such, as the four directions become more like 16.

Yes, I did find Scientifica in abundance there. But not in the ground. Every berry and branch was now in a sac carried by one man. "It's up to me to control this plant and what it does," this time," Stefan said to me. "With small portions to people I don't mind, bigger portions to those whom I like, and NONE of it to anyone else, including you."

"Why?" I asked him, in Equinese.

"Because a political system is only as good as the people, or person, in charge of it," his reply as he stepped towards me, his boots creating a bigger footprint somehow with each stride. "And that person is me," he declared, stroking me on the neck with a hand that felt like it belonged to someone else. "Us if you do as I command, ask and request from now on."

"Absolute power corrupts, absolutely," I thought, and had experienced on more than one occasion as the strongest and healthiest horse in at least five herds after my human soul had incarnated into the womb of the pregnant mare I had been riding, and to be truthful, abusing, as a human. I wanted to scream it at Stefan, but after ingesting an elephant-sized portion of Scientifica, he said it for me.

"Yes, absolute power corrupts absolutely," he declared. "But someone has to be on top, and someone on the bottom. And, you may ask, what determines in a noble society who is on top and who is on the bottom?"

"The cruel hand of Mother Nature or the merciful intervention of Spirit big S?" I snortled back.

"No!" Stefan screamed into my face, in the manner that his fellow Iankonians who didn't know my human origins did. "The person on top, or just below being on top, is measured by how effectively he unites those below him against a common enemy! That common enemy being…." .

"Who?" I snortled.

Lord and possibly executioner Stefan broke into mad laughter, which became a belly laugh that landed him on the ground, then catapulted him to his feet. After which, before I could anticipate his actions, he slipped a halter on me, jumped on my back, and kicked on my flanks. 'Forward!" he commanded.

This time, I didn't obey. I reared up, landing on my feet to find Philosopher-King Denosevic still on my back. My attempt to run with a ducked-down head resulted in Stefan anticipating this. He pulled my head upward, then turned me painfully to the left, into a circle that made my feet throb with pain, exhausting my lungs till I finally came to a stop. "Like I said," the man who was nothing like the one whom I had mentored and loved, whispered softly, pointing his pistol at my head. "Forward, please."

I obeyed him this time, moving forward at a collected trot, thinking with each step about how I could rectify the experiment I had set in motion. Hoping that the new puppeteer on my back was not reading my thoughts, and collecting them into a plan of action before I could.

# CHAPTER 18

"The rules in this game are simple," Stefan said to his hungover reunited dinner guests after waking them up from their beds with a breakfast of cold winter air on their naked chests, stripped of the tunics and coats that defined their political affiliation, along with and the medals and insignia which determined how valued they were by their bosses in Moscow, Washington, London, New York and Paris. "To your right, wolves in a cage are armed with sharp teeth and a healthy appetite for human meat," he said, moving towards an enclosure on the North side of the tavern. "To your left, up a steep hill, buried under a rock that no one man can uncover, your firearms, which you can use to kill these old and sick rabid wolves, each other or, if you want to---"

"---You?" Boyco blurted out, through the frost on his overgrown mustache. "Who stole our weapons and uniforms after putting something in the vodka other than alcohol?"

"You...still PRIVATE Denosevic, who insisted we toast each other for surviving the War," former Captain

Ivanov spat out of his mouth, doing his best not to show how cold and scared he was.

"And who locked us in the dining room, ordering us to put together a constitution that contradicted itself every other paragraph?" Melnyk grumbled.

"Then tricked us into signing 'birthday cards' that were actually papers that said we disagreed with everything the Army we were in stood for?" Koval stuttered from lips shaking with fear as well as cold.

"Which you said your brother will take to our leaders if we don't freely embrace your brand of government, Democratic Socialist-Christian-Libertarian King-Stefan," Sokolov pointed out, his hot rage making him oblivious to the cold. "Which is…"

"Something I haven't completely figured out yet," Stefan related, and confessed. "But I'm not a King, my potential friends, I am…"

"…a God now?'" Boyco blasted back. "Who promised to give 'the most worthy' of us Godlike powers? In a world where God doesn't exist anymore."

"But those who have guns do exist, Petrov," former Captain, now White Army Colonel Ivanov said, pointing the ex-Seargent and now Red Army Colonel to a row of Iankovian citizens of all ages and both genders appearing on the roofs around them as well as spectating from their balcony seats in the trees between the starting point of the race from the wolves, and the weapons under the heavy rocks.

"And maybe don't want to kill us, Boris?" Koval said, referring to his former commanding officer and now enemy combatant by his Christian name.

"But will," Melnyk added. "If their duly NON-elected President Denosevic says so. For…what, national security, Stefan?"

"Yes," Stefan replied, calmly. "A former village idiot who turned into something else has to do what he has to do."

"And how did that happen, Stefan?" Melnyk asked. "None of us will move from this spot in this gladiator game until you tell us, right?"

Four heads nodded 'yes' to the assertion, all at once. Stefan was pleased, putting a smile on his face. A kind one. But it seemed too kind.

"So?" Melnyk pressed. "If we play this game, you'll tell the survivors how and why you became who you are?"

"Yes, at the right time," Stefan said. "My hand to God!" he asserted, lifting his hand up. Of course I didn't believe him. "And on the eyes of my closest friend, and comrade," he said as he stroked my neck. I let myself believe that. Part of it anyway. "But, we're wasting time," he continued, after which he requested his son Sasha to hand him a stopwatch. On the count of ten, you, gentleman, run," the once young man said to the men who had been his superiors in command and worldly abilities. "And on the count of three, by necessity, they will," Stefan continued, pointing to the cage of growling wolves. "Fellow Citizens! From twenty!" Servant of the People, Stefan yelled to his loyal, and I hoped not drugged, blackmailed, or manipulated by fear or greed, fellow Iankovians.

The countdown echoed from one side of the village, each of the numbers melting into the other. On the count of ten, the gate holding in the five captive men was opened. With still unwet trousers, they ran into the woods, each slipping on the mud, the ones standing helping each other get up. Running towards the weapons with speed and determination as a team. As the countdown came to five, four then…

On the count of three, Stefan let the wolves out of their cage. On top of the hill, five men, bare to the waist, covered with mud, which made them all look like the same grunts in one army, held their weapons, aiming them at the wolves as they approached the woods. The men fired, their rounds replaced by blanks. Stefan whistled, causing the wolves to stop dead in their tracks. He said something in 'wolf' that seemed to be 'lunch time. ' The wild wolves turned into passive dogs, trotting back to Stefan, who rewarded them with chunks of dried beef from the saddlebag that was strapped on my back.

"You all passed, for now," Stefan announced to his dinner guests. "Andrei led a contingent of still armed Iankovians to the shivering compadres, bringing them their clothing. Insisting that each man wear an ensemble of wardrobe representing all of the ideologies.

"What if you didn't whistle to the wolves in time, and if they didn't help each other from the muck?" I thought and was about to give voice to it into Stefan's ear.

"Any objections to anything else I do, and it will be your meat in their mouths, by necessity," Stefan calmly whispered to me regarding the wolves who, prior to Stefan's 'education', indulged in a diet that consisted of domestic human and horse meat more than wild rabbit. "All by necessity, my friend," he continued. Making me think that it was safer being King Stefan's enemy than his friend. As I realized that the advancement of the mind is faster than that of the heart, the result is not effective compassion, but something else.

# CHAPTER 19

Stefan kept the last supply of Scientifica (that I knew about, anyway) in Ukraine, Russia, and most of the rest of Eastern Europe in a locked box in the Presidential Cabin built behind his house. To keep the elixor within the berries and leaves from breaking down, he devised a way to convert it to a powder which, when he tested it on himself, was even more potent than when it was found in its natural state. Through an open window in his cabin, which was viewable by only me and a few curious four legged onlookers in the woods behind me, I noted him putting the powder into neatly portioned bags labelled according to their weight, then placing them as if it was volatile dynamite, into what looked like a worn out treasure chest from the outside, secured with a padlock. One that was coated with a substance I could not identify, but, as tested by Stefan, would burn the hands of anyone who dared try to figure out the combination without gloves or a lot of time. The steel walls to the treasure chest were impenetrable by any weapon I knew about. And as for the toxin he put in various compartments around the combination lock, well, more than one rat who decided to much on it wound up as coyote meat with an exit from life with seizures that lasted an hour before it separated everything above the neck from below it.

Stefan kept a secret, ever-changing list of who would be given scientifica and in what doses. A key element in determining who got what involved setting up more various 'games' with the citizenry of his kingdom and the five soldiers from his past. One way to determine who would be more humane and effective at leading a coup against Stefan, thereby setting himself up as the common enemy. And of course, there were others equally as intricate as the one he played on, and for his five old Army buddies, the result was that they became Stefan's best friends. One of the people on the list of non-recipients of Scientifica was, as I expected, Svetlana. His wife, who, for reasons I could not understand, came to love Stefan more each day, while he fell into indifference to her with equal intensity at the same rate.

It wasn't that Stefan hated his wife, or considered Svetlana 'inferior'. Indeed, when I did see her making love to him, be it in bed with her still youthful and alluring body or with a special dish she had prepared, (the magical ingredient of 'love') converting even the simplest dishes she prepared into a gourmet meal worthy of any five star restaurant in Paris, or even with a smile after kissing him on the cheek, or lips, his 'thank you' smile was always forced. And, for all the wrong reasons, convincing to her. Perhaps he had outgrown the endorphin of love and was not addicted to the naturally manufactured, and highly addictive 'joy of discovery'. A 'joy' which had no element of happiness to it but..something else. Such is what I know happened to me after ingesting too much Scientifica in both human and animal form. Practicality trumped sentimentality, thinking loomed over feeling. Have-tos became infused with want-tos such that one could not tell the difference between the two. Made even more challenging when progressively higher 'Callings' came into the mix..

"A proper Cossack woman is a loving mother who will give us many sons and daughters," he would say of Svetlana as well as no less than 20 other Iankovian women who smiled 'good morning' to him while making the rounds in the village, which was as rich as any city in Europe. And more secure from invasion by any of the warring parties who wanted to inflict their ideology in the Russian Civil War than any country in the wilds of Siberia or canton in Switzerland. The physical fences around Iankovia involved everything from a network of deep pits covered with a thin layer of what seemed to be solid ground, to quicksand containing swamps provided by mother nature, to electrified wire that send a bolt of lightening into the brains of those who touched it, causing them to forget where they were, and who they were, as well as of course snipers hidden in trees who fired warning shots at unwelcomed intruders. There were also stories about Swiss-trained Professor Doctor Petrovitch and his students, who used lie detector machines to interview all refugees in need of shelter, medical aid, or food. They electrocuted anyone whose bleeding heart stories were found out to be false, their bodies fed to his lab rats. But, I getting back to the story that I intended to tell you, kind, gentle and I hope honest reader.

No one seemed to mind Stefan having several wives, and if they did, no one said anything about it. The many women in his life as a 'mature' adult, complete with pre-maturing grey hair in his warlock and overgrown mustache, who shunned him as an inferior lad five years ago all seemed to love him. But, who wouldn't love being made love to by a god? And one who somehow was able to give his flock everything they needed and wanted. Except for one thing…

"Free choice and an equal opportunity to be as intelligent and powerful as you can be, and deserve to be, you are thinking and are about to say, Achilles?" Stefan said to me on a 'pleasure ride' around the expanded borders of still oil, mineral, wheat, and livestock-rich Iankovia, inspecting the various new gates, fences, traps, and manufactured quicksand that kept dangerous people from coming in and useful ones from getting out. "Yes, I can read your thoughts now as well as or better than you were able to read mine," he continued, leaning down over the right side of my neck when he brought me to an abrupt halt after finishing his rounds.. . .

True, I did weigh five times more than Stefan did and was ten times more muscular, but it was he in (for the moment anyway) human form who had the most powerful of weapons. Hands that were able to grab things with an apposable thumb. An appendage that horses had lost as they evolved. Each time I figured out a way to toss him off my back, to take him on a run to where I thought he should go, his human hand pulled on the reins. Gone were the days when he would ask me at a fork in the road whether to go right or left. But gone would be Stefan and his dream for an Enlightened Iankovia, and by extension, an Enlightened world if I didn't do SOMETHING, particularly at this moment.

With eyes that could still see behind me, I noted something in his ocular portholes. A blank stare. Somehow, the visionary who said, most particularly to stagnant souls, 'the only real rest is in motion itself,' froze. His breathing was so faint that the cool air leaving his dropped jaw hadn't enough breath in it to turn into fog. .

I snortled, in the attempt to wake him up from whatever nightmare or demonic vision he was experiencing while still awake.

"I know," he replied. "Time to go home, or what used to be such anyway." With the lightest of touches, he nudged my flank. Letting me choose the course back to the windowless 'Presidential cabin' in back of his family's house."

For the first time since we met, Stefan was not a rider, but a passenger on my back. Passively letting me pick the route and the pace. I ambled along at a slow trot, sensing that he did have enough active brains in his ass to stay seated in the saddle. He muttered incoherent words and expletives that were not in any language I had spoken as a human or heard as a horse. Until I, and (in body anyway) he, arrived at our final destination.

A crowd was gathered there to greet Stefan. Every Iankovian who could emit a melodic note or blast out an off-key refrain from a wide smile sang "Happy Birthday" to Stefan, feeling happy, secure, and fulfilled. In love with each other, and even more so with Stefan. Perhaps they had a meeting and figured out that the games I played with and on them were FOR them. Their benefit, that is. Such now included all of his 'last war buddies and 'current war adversaries' who by some miracle had not yet killed each other due to their previous political affiliations. In response to such, Stefan woke up from his nightmare, and smiled in a way that convinced everyone walking on two rather than four legs that he was one of them. When he never could be one of them ever again.

I could, in that moment, feel and read his thoughts as he and I assessed where he was prior to the scientifica-induced transformation I inflicted on him, and afterwards. His vigilant gaze scanned every face in the singing, dancing, and adoring Iankovian crowd, which included, of course, many more 'immigrants' who considered themselves Iankoians. All sharing the Bliss of the Eternal Now. He worried about how this volcanic miraculous eruption of laughter and mirth could be sustained in the future.

I could hear his thoughts, which he also gave voice to, one matching the other word for word. "All I wanted when I was the village idiot, kept alive because I was a master surgeon and animal trainer who they needed for their material needs, was to be part of this magnificent family. I was banished then because of my never seeing the 'bad' in people. And now that I can see all the potential bad in people, and I am their leader, I am banished from being part of their family yet again." After a solemn deep breath of painful self-appraisal, he went on, still mounted, while looking at the corner of my eye. "Something that perhaps you, Achilles, experienced with every horse herd you joined or was conscripted to be in," came from his lips as he stroked my tired neck. "And maybe experienced as a human soul before you were forced into an animal body?"

I snortled back an affirmative and camaraderie 'yes' to all of the above. A bonding moment that was interrupted by Stefan diverting his gaze to something on the other side of an open window in his Presidential cabin.

"The lock on the most important treasure chest is on the floor now!" he grunted to me, restraining his voice. "Who opened it?"

His perusal of the faces in the adoring collection of citizenry turned sinister. His attention went on and into every soul present, the accusatory thoughts behind his mind-reading brain remaining hidden to everyone present. As, no doubt, he considered who was absent. Or who had become a better mind reader and 'bad thought' reader than he was, courtesy of what had been in the old treasure chest reinforced to become a small vault. The one containing not gold, silver, coins, or diamonds but Scientifica, the last supply of such that was present in Ukraine and the rest of what had been the Russian Empire, to the best of my knowledge and experience anyway.

"Stefan, come join the dance in your honor, my love!" his wife Svetlana exclaimed. She meant every word of it, despite the fact that she doubt knew that at least ten other women had shared their bed, and heart, with him.

"Yes! Join the dance!" everyone else gave voice to.

Stefan faked his most convincing smile, saying to the crowd, "Yes, after I evacuate my bowels and bladder. And change my boots so I don't step on everyone's feet! And retrieve the gift that I prepared for all of YOU on this special day!" he proclaimed. He dismounted, then strolled with wide strides, being sure not to let anyone see him run in desperation towards the cabin. His back turned to the adoring crowd, but not to me; his smile turned into a hate-infused grimace. Primal rage entered his entire being after he opened the door and entered the 'office', which no one was allowed entry to, gently closing the door behind him.

I remained outside of course, edging my way to an open window, discreetly looking at Stefan when he didn't think I had eyes on him. After putting on a pair of gloves, he picked up the padlock from the floor. Then opened the chest that was unopenable.

It was gone! All of the Scientifica that Stefan had collected. His bridled rage turned into primal fear.

It is said that the response to a wild animal, or worse, ferocious fellow human, when your inner or outer life is threatened, is fight or flight. Wolves do the former. We horses usually do the latter. What Stefan did next was a terrifying combination of both.

# CHAPTER 20

Wearing new boots that wouldn't injure any feet he accidentally stepped on with his now completely music-less feet, Stefan filled a "Santa bag" with money, jewels, and top-dollar ancient trinkets, along with exotic foods, placing them in the communal pot for the fund to "Enrich, Enlighten, and Educate Iankovia now—and the rest of the world very, very soon."

He was offered and returned hugs while watching—and hearing, though not quite listening to—the orchestra of fiddles, mandolins, and drums. The crowd was so large that the faces blurred before him. He called it a surprise boost to the local economy, an early "tax refund." Together, he and I watched the citizens—people who had truly given what they could in service—take from the communal pot for their needs, and a few forgivable wants.

Theoretically, those who took the smallest portions were already rich—at least in their minds—thanks to the *Scientifica* they had either purposefully or accidentally ingested. That was our working hypothesis, anyway.

There was no shortage of suspects when it came to who had broken into, or indulged in, Stefan's most valued treasure chest. There wasn't a single person in Ivankovia whom "Citizen Comrade President" Stefan hadn't intimidated, tricked, or blackmailed into being a better version of themselves.

Theoretically, it was only me, a few well-fed frogs, birds, field mice—and Stefan—who knew the true power of *Scientifica*: its ability to catapult anyone from the bottom of the social pyramid straight to the top. But as we all know—or should know—the most obvious theories are often the ones that prove themselves wrong. Especially at the worst possible times.

From several vantage points, I watched my somehow-still-best-friend celebrate what was now deemed the first annual *Feast of Saint Stefan*. And for the first time, I saw something new in his face. Not fear exactly, but paranoia— the creeping suspicion of being outmatched by someone who had taken too much *Scientifica*. Someone who could *see* Stefan's darkest secrets... even the ones he hid from himself.

Every citizen was now a suspect. And if word got out about what *Scientifica* could really do, Iankovia was in danger. The once-isolated village, now teeming with refugees from Ukraine, Poland, Russia, and Turkey, had become its own small country. But maybe—just maybe— everyone had partaken of the elixir and been turned into super-geniuses.

That would push Stefan back down to the bottom of the intellectual totem pole—an "average" genius. And if the horses had some mixed into their hay nets, I'd be down there with him.

Yet, as we scanned the gathering, there were no signs. No darting eyes, no light-emitting auras—the telltale signs of *Scientifica*. Maybe the real question wasn't who *was* at the Feast, but who *wasn't*. And who had been closest to Stefan during his dealings beyond Iankovia.

"Yes, I know. My brother, Andre," Stefan said to me, as the crowd, now drunk or danced into blissful exhaustion, settled down. "The one I sent on an assignment. The one who's late. My older—and back when we were kids, smarter and more clever—brother who—"

"—Is not here," I snortled.

"And he used to say to me, more than once and in different ways," Stefan continued quietly, "Every time you go on a private walkabout to your favorite secret place in the woods, you come back more distant from the rest of us."

He sighed. "And when he saw the list of people I was considering for official positions of power and influence, he asked why he wasn't on it. I told him, *I don't want you burdened and cursed with what's happened to me.*"

Then came the line I'd heard him say before, wrapped in a proverb masquerading as a joke: "*Anyone who wants to be President of any country shouldn't be trusted with the job."*

With that, Stefan took a deep breath, lifted his trembling chin, and placed a bridle on me. He led me to the corral where his Army buddies' horses were finishing the last of the special rum Mrs. Lubinska had reserved for her return to a now-free Poland.

A buzzed—but not yet drunk—Boyco passed the jug to a still teetotaling Stefan, encouraging him to indulge. "It's a special occasion," he said. "Even Jesus drank wine."

Stefan sniffed, then took a sip… and three hefty gulps, earning applause and a chorus of *atta boys* from his comrades.

Then he leaned in and whispered to me, "Doctor Lubinska gave them a placebo. They think they're drunk—but thankfully, especially today, they aren't."

He called over his sober son, Sasha, who was wearing the apron of the *all-your-body-needs-but-not-what-your-palate-wants* outdoor kitchen.

"So," Sasha said, eyes bright, "you're finally going to let me see, experience, and transform the world?" He pulled off his apron and cap, revealing a freshly shaved head and a Cossack warlock braid identical to his father's—minus the grey hairs.

"You're not quite ready for the world, Sasha," Stefan replied gently, resting a hand on his son's shoulder. "And maybe... the world isn't quite ready for *you*, as you are now."

Sasha growled, about to speak. From his look, I guessed he was ready to unleash a storm about being just as skilled as his father—as a surgeon, a horse trainer, and a faithful executor of divine providence.

But before he could say a word, Stefan cut him off.

"Yes, I know what you're thinking—and feeling. But I need someone I can trust here. Someone I love, in my own twisted way. And right now, Sasha, I need you to temporarily reactivate those skills you used to get top grades back in the day."

"Which are?" Sasha asked, calming.

"Forging papers," Stefan answered. "Five sets. Written with help from my Army comrades. You'll tell them to report back here in three hours, looking exactly as they did when they first arrived—on the outside, anyway. Inside, of course, they're changed men."

"Because of you," Sasha added. "Why?"

"So we can trade places—captors for prisoners, prisoners for captors," Stefan replied. He looked in all four directions—north, south, east, and west—then back north, eyes sweeping the ground and the bush for tracks. Finally, he turned to Sasha. "I think I know where your Uncle Andre went. But I don't know who else is with him... or who's encroaching on our borders because of him—or despite him."

"…Sometimes we have to pretend to be who we're not," Sasha said, completing the lesson, "so we can become, in the long run, who we really are?"

"Yes!" Stefan grinned. "Yes, my finally true Cossack son!"

He pulled Sasha into a bear hug—faster and harder than Sasha could return.

"Now," the Old Professor said to the young Warrior-Healer, "tell my war buddies: no one must know about this mission. I need you to be…"

"…The man of the house," father and son said in unison, though their voices rang with very different notes.

"I'll be back in an hour," Stefan said, scanning the hoofprints of Andre's specially shoed mare, Natasha. I sniffed at the traces of her elusive, seductive *Equinos Elusiva* scent—not sure if I was using my nostrils or my imagination.

"I'll check the perimeter of our still-not-destroyed country," he said. "And if I'm not back in an hour—send the guys after me, son," my 'master' said, as we trotted on.

# CHAPTER 21

I never knew if it was Andrei or Stefan who had insisted that Natasha be given specially designed horseshoes—ones that could grip ice without letting snow build up in her hooves. Whoever it was, the decision made it easy for Stefan and his Great War comrades to follow her tracks after we crossed the northern border of Iankovia.

That border, newly extended, now absorbed two neighboring villages—both recently burned out of existence by the roaming armies who chased each other across the countryside, killing more civilians than enemy combatants. Natasha's trail led us toward the weathered road bearing the sign:

"Welcome to Iankovia. Where you must leave political ideology, personal greed, and tortured pasts behind."

Next to the sign stood an overflowing garbage bin stuffed with torn propaganda leaflets, a few discarded crucifixes, and several shredded wedding photographs.

Mother Nature contributed her defenses too—thick woods and swamps still impassable in deep winter. But

Iankovia's new "Security Department" had added their own: fresh fences and booby-trapped pits designed to dissuade unwelcome guests. Remarkably, they were still intact. And then there were the sharpshooters—perched in treehouses—under orders to aim for the feet of intruders or the tires of any vehicle daring to approach on the few broken paths connecting Iankovia to the rest of the world.

Today was another "high security alert" day. A hundred yards behind the "Welcome" sign and two hundred before reaching the oil fields, bountiful farmland, and mineral mines, bold signs read:

"SPANISH FLU EPIDEMIC – ENTER AT YOUR OWN RISK."

Black flags flapped for the benefit of the still-plentiful illiterate pirates, rogue soldiers, and self-declared generals. The sight of military boot prints marching in perfect formation—followed by chaotic trails all around them—suggested that psychological warfare was working better than bullets ever could.

As we passed through, Stefan gave a respectful bow to the treehouse snipers, a gesture of thanks for their continued vigilance. He was dressed as always in loose blue trousers, hand-stitched leather boots, and his grandfather's black *cherkeska* coat. His wild mustache and foot-long warlock braid swayed in the breeze, a colorful tribute to the free-spirited Cossack armies of old. Behind him rode his Great War comrades, dressed head to toe in the drab, functional uniforms of the political affiliations they once served—before being lured to Iankovia by Andrei's invitation.

Each man rode the same horse he had arrived on. But now, the horses' thoughts—formerly concerned with food, sleep, and mating—had shifted to confusion about the intentions of their now-transformed riders.

"Remember, lads," Stefan said, guiding his mount across Natasha's fading hoofprints, the border now far behind us, "if you see anyone else wearing those freshly cleaned and pressed uniforms you now have on, understand this:

You are no longer deserters—you're returnees. And we, the rest of us, are your captured converts. Prisoners, yes, but also carriers of valuable intelligence. If we encounter a captain, say the information is meant for a major. If it's a major, say a colonel. A colonel? Then we demand a general. And if it's a general—"

"—God?" Ivanov interjected, clutching the cross beneath his White Army tunic.

"Or Hetman Denosevic?" added Boyco, the Red Army major once proudly atheist, now rethinking everything.

"He *may* exist," Stefan allowed with a dry smile.

"And he did suggest one golden rule," said Melmyk, the anarchist with the stark white face beneath an all-black uniform stitched with chaotic individuality. "Do unto others as you'd have them do unto you."

"Which doesn't work so well globally if you're a masochist," Koval added, wearing a civilian suit pinned with flags of all the countries eager to 'cure' Russia— provided they could colonize it. The Stars and Stripes were most prominent.

"You're all wrong," said Sokolov, the former opportunist and freelance partisan. He glanced down at the string of scalps, ears, and eyes hidden under his coat— souvenirs no one in Iankovia wanted to buy, or even acknowledge. "The real power lies with the one holding the biggest gun. Or the craftiest mind. It's survival of the fittest. Jungle law. Steppe law. It's not about *us*. It's about *me*. And what's to stop me from turning around, putting a bullet in *you*, 'Hetman Denosevic,' and taking everything you've built for myself?"

"Your disbelief in what you just said," Stefan answered coolly. "And the fact that during the War, you saved all our lives—mine included—at least five times. At your own risk."

"Yeah, but you were all family then," Sokolov muttered.

"And now," Stefan replied, "so are the people of Iankovia. You, too, are part of that family. You proved it— even if at first, you were only a blackmailed guest. And speaking of family," he added with a wry grin, "I've seen how you look at my daughter Tanya. And how she smiles back at you."

"I know," Sokolov said, lowering his eyes—eyes now soft and filled with something deeper than lust. "She's too young for me. So I'll—"

"—Propose to her in a few years," Stefan interrupted firmly, "when she's old enough to tell the difference between love and infatuation—and wise enough to choose the former."

"And when you'll need one of those scalps to cover your balding head," Koval teased.

"I'm not—" Sokolov gasped, instinctively rubbing the back of his head. "I can't be—"

"Genetics, my friend," Koval said with a shrug. "Your father. Your grandfather. It's inevitable."

"Nicholi! Petro! Vladimir!" Sokolov called, turning to Ivanov, Boyco, and Melmyk. "It's still there, right? Tell me my hair's still all there!"

Guided by a mischievous wink from Koval, all three men gave vague, negative answers. Sokolov paled and turned back to Stefan.

"You, Hetman. Stefan. I know I ridiculed you, long ago. But you never lied to me, not once. Even when I lied to you. So… what do *you* see?" he asked, positioning himself in front of me, baring his head.

Stefan paused, then said evenly, "I see someone standing in front of my horse during a mission we need to keep moving. Or we'll all fall backward into a very deep abyss."

He let the silence settle before adding: "But I will tell you a secret no one else in Iankovia knows yet."

"What secret?" Sokolov asked, eyes wide.

"Yes, tell us," Boyco pressed, hand resting on his pistol.

Melmyk, Koval, and Ivanov tensed, fingers brushing against triggers.

Stefan looked into each man's eyes, reading truths that perhaps he hadn't dared see before. And then he burst into laughter—mad, unrestrained laughter. He laid his hand on Sokolov's shoulder.

"My most beloved and trusted son-in-law," he announced, spinning his warlock braid like a banner. "Tanya loves *this*"—he pointed to the braid—"and *especially this!*" he added, rubbing his freshly shaven, still-hirsute head.

"Really?" Sokolov asked, hopeful.

"Really, Dmitri," Stefan said, the warmth in his voice unmistakable. He was speaking not just as a comrade or leader—but as a father. A father five years younger than his future son-in-law, yet now looking twenty years older.

Stefan nodded with affection and authority. "Now, I ask you—take your place in line, and let's proceed."

"Yes, Stefan," Sokolov said. Then corrected himself: "I mean… Hetman."

"Dad," Stefan said. "Very soon."

He hugged Sokolov tightly and kissed both his cheeks.

I asked the horse beneath Sokolov what he thought of all this. His answer came back, calm and clear:

"Something very good. For now."

And I was reminded of a truth I rarely shared with anyone:

Sometimes, choosing *not* to look too deeply into someone's mind or soul allows you—rightly or wrongly—to work with them. To play with them. To trust them, even if you shouldn't.

Sokolov resumed his place in line, and we moved forward.

What Stefan planned to do with Andrei—his own brother, who, interestingly, was not on the final list of those selected to receive *Scientifica*—was unknown. Perhaps, as Stalin once put it, Andrei was on his way to becoming a "useful idiot" for Stefan's cause. But as history has shown, idiots with even a pinch of power or intelligence eventually stop being useful and start becoming dangerous.

I recalled the fleeting three-second glance I'd had at Stefan's secret list. The five men riding behind me *were* on it—destined for earthly promotion and a measured dose of *Scientifica*.

As long as they didn't know it... I suppose that was a good plan.

# CHAPTER 22

Andrei's exit from Iankovia—astride a horse groaning under his overly fed, fat ass and burdened with the sac of *Scientifica*—led us through territories of all shades and flags. In Red-controlled zones, Boyko proudly proclaimed that he had captured Whites and Anarchists, along with a demented, quixotic old Cossack mental patient: an incoherent, babbling Stefan who knew the terrain far better than he knew how to communicate with any human on it.

The prematurely bald, Western businessman-clad Koval managed to pass himself off as Vladimir Lenin's semi-legitimate son—not yet old enough to grow a proper goatee—when we were intercepted in Bolshevik territory. There, he received letters from both loyal and disgruntled Red Army soldiers, offering suggestions on how to make the transition to Bolshevik Communism more palatable to the counter-revolutionary masses. One letter proposed allowing Spirituality to remain in Russia—but without the shackles of organized, dictatorial religion. It was a sentiment Stefan had championed long before the February Revolution of 1917—or the second one, in that same year that, all things considered, now seemed almost longed for again.

In regions controlled by the Whites, the "captured after deserting and seeing a vision of the Virgin Mary" born-again Christian Red Army Major Boyko—now wearing Ivanov's cross—sang praises to Jesus, interspersed with curses branding Lenin as the Antichrist.

In areas overseen by the American Expeditionary Forces, "The Star-Spangled Banner" was sung in both Russian and accent-laden English by Koval, who was en route to Poland with prisoners he claimed to have single-handedly captured—and converted into "grateful servants of Yankee Capitalism." Delivered with convincing flair to the well-armed yet pathetically inexperienced American Doughboys, Koval's rhetoric found eager ears. These young Americans had lingered in Europe after the November 11, 1918 Armistice, lured by promises of higher pay, a taste for adventure, patriotic zeal to halt the Red Terror—or simply a desire to delay returning to the humdrum lives of farmers, factory workers, and "wholesome family men" across the Atlantic.

Melmyk, newly adorned with the self-bestowed rank of Anarchist Captain—in an army theoretically without rank—explained to the checkpoint guards in black that each Anarchist had the right to decide for himself, and that his current 'experiment' involved deprogramming Reds, Whites, and Expeditionary soldiers, as well as civilians too afraid of a world without laws, statues, and civic orders. His passage was granted, mostly due to a generous offering of coins, jewels, and gold nuggets—a contribution to the noble cause of eliminating rigid, oppressive systems, whether they hailed from Reds, Whites, Americans, or Ukrainian Pirates disguised as Nationalists when it suited their purposes.

By the end of the day, we had covered at least fifty miles—according to the odometer in my aching feet. The trail of Andrei's mare grew more distinctive after we crested a steep hill, leading into a high-country meadow where brown grass strained to push through frozen mud. For every three shallow hoofprints from Natasha, there was one that was deep. Our Hetman suddenly stopped, crouching to examine the ground more closely.

"Natasha's lame on the left front," Stefan noted, referring to Andrei's horse with more compassion than he ever offered to me—or anyone else. "And when she was running the last three miles, she was working with her right lead instead of her left. Which means…"

"We're finally closing in on your once-trusted Andrei?" Boyko asked, weariness heavy in his voice.

"Yes, there's that," Stefan acknowledged, as if it were a secondary concern. "But it also means Andrei is not the man he was a few days ago. Or a year ago. He'd never push Natasha—or any horse—past its limits. Unless…"

"He's desperate?" Boyko offered.

"He's drunk?" Koval guessed.

"He's possessed by the Devil," Ivanov interjected, crossing himself. "A devil that exists—for reasons only God knows."

"A God who maybe still wants us to follow *some* rules," Melmyk added, glancing skyward, "so we can be free of being ruled by others? Even 'liberators' who think they *are* God?" he shot toward Stefan with purpose.

"Who promised us positions of worldly power and influence if we followed him on a wild goose chase to find his older, more likable brother?" Sokolov added. "A brother who—"

"—May have been *transformed* into someone less likable by…" Stefan allowed himself to suggest.

"Something he ate, maybe?" Boyko ventured.

Stefan froze. He had told no one but me about *Scientifica*, nor of the list detailing who was meant to receive that potion from the gods—one that, in small doses, turned mortals into clairvoyant cynics; in larger ones, rulers; and in rare excess, kings.

"Yes," Stefan finally said, slowly preparing himself to reveal what he never intended to share. He would soon offer his once-trusted war comrades positions in the new Iankovian Parliament—and its to-be-formed Army, designed to protect the nation's fragile new existence. "Something that…"

"—Came from Oksana's magic bag of potions," Boyko interrupted. "Oksana the—"

"—Gypsy mandolin player and singer," Koval added. "A refugee from Lithuania who found a home in Iankovia all too quickly. And easily."

"A home visited by deserving men in search of affections they can't get from their wives, children, dogs, or horses," Sokolov said. "So they don't abandon their families or eat their stubborn animals."

"Yes, dear Oksana," Ivanov added with acid. "Who, for a price, uses the devil's witchcraft—herbs in tea after receiving their seed in her bed—to turn saints into sinners, then into instruments of cruelty. With that special cherry-flavored brandy she keeps for *special guests*, beside a bed that smells like lilacs and feels like silk."

"Which you seem to know quite a bit about, former Captain, then Major, now aspiring Mayor of Moscow, Ivanov," Boyko fired back. "When the Whites take over, of course."

Stefan's old war comrades exchanged secrets about "Director of Music and Dance" Oksana in a strange camaraderie—half gossip, half confession. It was a kind-hearted sharing of stories, part fact, part fiction, and part personal memory. Stefan—despite, or perhaps because of, his growing intellect and political power—had never slept with Oksana. Hearing the stories, he took deep breaths of relief. His original plan remained intact: to sneak carefully rationed doses of *Scientifica* into the tea of the militarily most seasoned men in Iankovia—without their knowledge.

Yes, seeing the five men laugh together was a rare and welcome sight. They deserved it. Stefan, however, had no room for levity. He had sacrificed laughter, joy, and fleeting happiness for a higher reward: accomplishment, stained with a kind of inner, privately savored bliss.

"Gentlemen?" Hetman Stefan said, after he and I had silently shared in the moment of levity. "It is time to proceed—so we can catch Andrei before he does any more damage to himself, his horse, or the world." He spoke carefully, yet again avoiding the imperative tense. He was inviting them to share his Vision—on his terms.

It was the last 'order' Stefan gave until…

# CHAPTER 23

Natasha's hoofprints disappeared beneath low-lying brush that choked the only trail through woods too dense for man or beast to chart their own direction. But the winding path she'd been forced along remained obvious—disturbed twigs and snapped branches coated with stray brown hairs from Natasha's wide hips, long mane, and her flagging tail—raised like a proud Arab's when she trotted. Blood tinged her fur, and sweat clung to every strand. Whether those fluids were human or equine, I couldn't tell. My nostrils were already overwhelmed by the stench of my own sweat and the scent of the horses trailing behind me, trudging through the tight trail in single file.

As if she *wanted* to be followed—or rescued—Natasha occasionally left a trail of manure. I remembered our strange conversations during the rare moments Andrei and Stefan gave us reprieve. She would turn her ass toward me, vulva open, drop a pile, and in her most melodic voice say: *"No pain, no gain. Walk through the path I'm laying down. What you seek—what your soul aches for—will be found."*

Yes, equine poetry has its quirks.

We couldn't see the sky. The warmth and light of the bright sun faded as we pressed deeper into the forest. The canopy of pine-needle-laced branches formed an impenetrable roof over our aching heads. Stefan, again, pulled his compass from his coat and whispered to me— only me—"North keeps changing on us." The needle pointed one direction, then shifted as soon as he looked again. "If we're going in circles," he added, "so is Andrei. And if you—"

He stopped mid-sentence. Boyko's horse had bumped into my ass—whether at the behest of his rider or one of the horsefly-sized gnats feasting on the gelding's flank, I didn't know.

"I didn't hear what you said, Hetman Comrade President," Boyko called forward. "Maybe the rest of us can—"

Stefan silenced him with a blistered finger pressed to the tip of his nose, then gestured with the silent hand signals we'd all learned in the Great War. Move forward. Quietly. Quickly.

Boyko passed it down the line.

The goat path—narrow and deceptively inviting at the entrance—ended after five more minutes of the darkest, most exhausting forest trek I could remember. Finally, sunlight warmed our backs. We emerged into a secluded meadow: lush green grass, a clear stream, and there, grazing freely, Natasha—riderless, blood-slicked flanks glistening.

Her hindquarters faced us, open in invitation. A *"come hither, stud or proud cut gelding"* offered to the world. For a brief, shameful moment, I considered obliging her. Maybe she still longed to be bred, even if the sperm sac in the horse my soul now inhabited had been removed and served up as prairie oysters to hungry veterinarians—or as steak tartare to their dogs.

My fantasy was shattered by five thunderous rifle cracks behind us.

Stefan snapped my neck around faster than I could on my own—and I was a horse trained to run *toward* danger. The horses behind us were now riderless, galloping away. On the ground lay four bodies. Motionless. Boyko, however, writhed, howling for his mother, limbs twitching, blood soaking the grass.

"Damn it. I *hate* when I miss," came a voice from above.

Perched on a tree branch, Sasha handed a sleek rifle— custom-built for Andrei—to his trembling father.

"Maybe you should finish him off?" he said, coldly.

"Help me! Please! I can't see! I can't feel my legs or arms!" Boyko screamed.

"So I *did* hit the optic chiasm," Sasha said smugly. "Then the ventral thalamic nucleus... Right, Professor Doctor Denosivic?" He handed the rifle to Stefan. "Your turn, Father Fearest. Hit the centromedian thalamus. Shut off the breathing center. And if you're *really* skilled, the heart."

Stefan took the rifle. The first shot deepened Boyko's agony. The second ended it. The third pierced his heart.

"Three shots?" Sasha mocked. "With all that biologically enhanced intelligence, you should've managed one. Very disappointing, *Stefan*."

It was the first time I'd heard Sasha address his father by first name—and he used the exact words Stefan had so often used when Sasha had failed in surgery or stumbled in the library.

Stefan's eyes circled wildly—over Boyko's corpse, inward to his own guilt, upward toward God, downward to the Devil, and finally to Sasha's smug, unrepentant face.

Then, with trembling resolve, he pointed the rifle at his son.

"Yes. *Very* predictable," Sasha said, voice dry with disdain.

Stefan pulled the trigger.

Nothing.

Sasha laughed—a sound I had never heard from him before. Joyless. Mocking.

Stefan reached for his own gunbelt, fumbling bullets into the chamber of Andrei's rifle, jamming it.

"Impossible," Sasha said with mock sympathy. "Since *I* altered Andrei's gun." He flicked hidden switches and fired three precise rounds into the sky.

Then he pointed it at me.

"No!" Stefan cried, stepping between us. "Achilles didn't do anything to you!"

"But he did something to *you*," Sasha replied, eyes narrowing. "I don't know how yet... but I saw him lead *you* to that patch of berries. The *magic* ones."

"Andrei told you?"

"After some... persuasion." Sasha grinned. "Then I had to put him out of his misery."

"Like you're about to do to me?" Stefan asked, broken but still standing.

"You didn't include *me* on your list," Sasha hissed. "Your list of worthy ones—recipients of those sacred berries. The ones that turn pathologically optimistic fools into philosophers who see the rot beneath the surface. That, in higher doses, make gods out of slaves... and obedient sons into something more. Something divine."

"And what do you want from me now?" Stefan asked.

"And why?" he added after a pause.

Sasha paced among the bodies, letting the question simmer in the air. Then, after a long silence, he stopped.

"To the first... I'll let you know when I want something."

"And the second?" Stefan pressed.

Sasha shrugged. "Maybe one day you'll understand. Or maybe you won't."

He tossed his father a heavy pack. Then slung a larger duffel bag onto my back.

"You two walk," he said coldly, climbing onto Natasha's back. "*I* ride."

He dug Andrei's spurs into her sides.

And off we went—again.

# CHAPTER 24

I didn't know where we were going—only that Sasha was leading the way. He pushed Stefan and me past warring factions: Reds, Whites, Anarchists, Nationalists, and Expeditionary Forces. Evidence of their passage lay all around us—burned villages, rotting corpses, blank-eyed refugees, and a new scourge introduced by this civil war: buried, unused artillery shells that exploded when stepped on the wrong way. No doubt they would be refined for the next war to end all wars.

"A shame you didn't put those landmines into your defense system around Ivankovia. But I will," Sasha said as we crossed the fourth such field, nearly setting off an explosion that would have solved all my problems—and Stefan's current dilemma.

"'Mine fields.' *MINE* field. *Mine*. A joke," the self-declared king of our newborn country announced. "You're supposed to laugh at my jokes, the way you expected me to laugh at yours, Stefan," the son reminded the father.

"Yes. It is a clever witticism," the deposed Hetman replied.

Sasha drew his whip and lashed it across Stefan's back. The third strike was painful enough to force a chuckle from the old man. Sasha responded with another scar, commanding him to laugh louder. Stefan obeyed. The whip stopped. The pain didn't—it had only changed form. Now it was the agony of defeat and surrender.

"That's being a good lad," Sasha said, by way of a compliment. "So you shall be rewarded—"

He tossed an apple to Stefan, whose growling, empty stomach cried out to devour it. Yet whether out of compassion or defiance, Stefan offered it to me. Why I accepted it, I still don't know. Perhaps to save him from the irony of consuming an apple offered by a demon—like the one in the Eden story. Or maybe I believed it was his turn to suffer—to atone for what others would call sins, and what a non-believer might simply call "miscalculations."

Among those miscalculations: trusting Andrei with the "extra benefits" of Scientifica berries, assuming his brother could be cajoled or intimidated into keeping it secret. Another was excluding Sasha from the ranks of "the chosen"—those secretly given rationed doses of Scientifica so their elevated intelligence could guide the rest with effective compassion. A third was believing that Sasha had inherited a strong, kind heart from his father, rather than a weak—and therefore dangerous—one from his mother.

There were other miscalculations, too. But the most damning was this: violating the sacred law Stefan himself had preached to all Ivankovians—to listen to others with an open heart and thinking mind, and to place yourself in their shoes before doing anything *to* them or *for* them.

What Stefan—and until now, I—had failed to grasp was that those granted the advanced intelligence Scientifica produced began to view themselves, perhaps rightly, as a different species from ordinary or even exceptional humans. But was that a sin? A miscalculation? Not of intention, perhaps. After all, a human being—with a larger brain and an opposable thumb—cannot truly "get into the head or heart" of a dog, a mouse, or a cockroach. At least not most of the time.

# CHAPTER 25

Sasha, seated comfortably on an abandoned cart with his horse, Natasha, tethered behind it, looked every inch the new Hetman of our fledgling country. He took his time pushing Stefan and me forward, keeping us in harness. A rifle was trained on our backs, ready to fire a torrent of lead—or darts containing "special medication"—should we try to escape. The darts, he warned, were designed to inflict the most damage on whichever of us ran slowest.

The road home was at least eight times longer—both in time and pain—than the one that led us to the so-called father-son reunion. I measured it in the ache of my legs and the holes that had worn into Stefan's boots. Sasha claimed the meandering route—the "curves that are the shortest distance between two points"—was to avoid being caught, killed, or conscripted by the Red, White, and Black armies or the Expeditionary Forces. That part, he delivered on. How he knew where they all were, neither Stefan nor I could guess.

When Stefan finally asked how he knew where not to go, Sasha replied, "You'll find out when you get home.

Where you'll enjoy an uneventful retirement. A well-fed retirement. You'll eat what I give you—and you'll like it."

Whether that meant confinement on stale bread and stagnant water, or house arrest with a feast of stew made from *my* flesh, I wasn't sure. But I was certain of this: something had gone terribly wrong with our theories about Scientifica.

According to Socrates, ignorance was the sole cause of cruelty—so greater intelligence should lead to greater compassion. But maybe it's not the seed that determines the tree, but the soil it finds itself in—and the genetics of the seed. Genetics, in this case, that came partly from Svetlana, Stefan's manipulative wife, and partly from Andrei, Stefan's brother. A man who only behaved morally when blackmailed or threatened with divine punishment by a post-Scientifica Stefan who once embodied God to him. A God Stefan no longer believed in—until now, when he prayed with a fervor and remorse that exceeded anything I'd ever witnessed.

"You are now a servant of *me*, not God," Sasha reminded him, whenever Stefan's muffled prayers grew loud enough to be heard despite the bit in his mouth. He enforced the point with a crack of his whip across Stefan's back—or, if Stefan refused to quiet down, across my own.

Eventually, we reached the northern perimeter of Ivankovia. Sasha pulled back the reins on our mouths and the harnesses on our chests.

"The guards in the trees—the ones who give warning shots? Where are they?" Stefan asked boldly.

"In town," Sasha said with pride. "Getting paid in money, vodka, and cheap whores. Not with admiration and respect, like *you* thought they wanted."

"There are no whores in Ivankovia. Not the kind that give even an ounce of satisfaction without a pound of genuine love, anyway," Stefan replied. "And vodka is forbidden. As for money, everyone here gives according to their abilities and receives according to their needs—and morally sound wants that don't hurt anyone else. And I set up—"

"—A country that no longer exists," Sasha cut in. "Not the way *you* built it. Or intended to build it. With your specially rationed doses of Scientifica for the 'loving elite' on that secret list of yours. Those people are now... well."

"The ones who are *not* getting Scientifica," Stefan growled, "while those with black hearts like yours are getting *all* of it?"

"Only what I want them to have. What I *need* them to have," Sasha replied, smug. "With the help of someone you don't need to know about. Just enough to make them smart enough to do what they're told. Useful idiots, compared to me. And for a little while, compared to you and that horse of yours."

He paused. "By the way, the name you gave me at birth was *Alexander*—a conqueror's name. That's what you'll call me now. *Professor Doctor Emperor Alexander the Greatest.* Not Sasha, the introspective little obedient son you once thought you raised."

"And your horse, Natasha, Alexander?" Stefan asked, eyeing the mare who, thankfully, no longer bore her new master's weight. "Andrei's horse, the one who loved him. Who carried him up and down the harshest terrain, through the worst conditions, and—"

"—Now serves *me*," Alexander snapped. He turned to the mare, pointed to his knife, then at her, then rubbed his belly with mock hunger. "And if she doesn't, well…" He laughed maniacally. "Too stupid to know what I'm saying, anyway!"

Natasha, her body already marked with whip scars, did not seem to understand his words—but she sensed something. The once independent, stubborn mare—who had never been ruled by any stallion and often ruled them instead—was afraid. She looked at me, her eyes begging me to save her.

I responded in horse-speak, in telepathy, in the language of silent promises: *Yes, of course. I have a plan.*

I hoped she couldn't tell I was lying.

# CHAPTER 26

In our absence, Iankovia had reverted to what it once was—and, according to the laws of natural selection, perhaps what it was always destined to become. A "simple" place where oil rigs pumped black gold at full speed, turning the once-blue sky into a putrid, choking fog. The mountains had been raped of their gold, silver, coal, and copper, with no regard for what once lived on their slopes. The wheat fields were stripped bare—nothing left to grow, nothing left to harvest.

The expanded hospital and university had been converted into a slaughterhouse, where anything deemed "defective" or of immediate utility—whether walking on four legs or, perhaps, two—was processed into sausages, spiced to ensure the source of the meat was indistinguishable. The newly built and generously stocked library had, in our absence, become a brothel. Its madam? Svetlana, Stefan's wife. Her most prized and genuinely willing—and undeniably attractive—"pleasure provider" was Tanya, 'Prime Minister Alexander's' own sister. Upon our return 'home,' mother and daughter were dressed in the latest Parisian fashions, adorned with no shortage of jewels around their necks and wrists.

Across the street from the ever-full tavern stood a new laundry shop. The lowest person on the totem pole—struggling to scrub blood from the military uniforms of fallen Red, White, and Black Army soldiers, along with the garments of the Expeditionary Forces and their civilian advisors—was none other than...

"Mrs. Lubinska?" Stefan said softly to the white-haired woman, her pale skin blotched with bruises in red, black, and blue. Her eyes were downturned, her spirit visibly broken.

"The ex-Professor of Ethics, Morals, and Literature," Alexander interjected, smirking. "The one foolish enough to consider *you* her favorite student. Now learning a new craft—just as she always said..."

He turned to the old woman who had once done her best to teach him, back when he was still Sasha.

"'Every scientist should know how to be a shoemaker, and every egotistical scholar should learn to be a laundress.' So she can earn the right to be called by her last name again. Right, *Evey*?" he added, sneeringly invoking the bastardized nickname she was mocked with by class clowns during her thankless tenure as teacher of the mostly unteachable.

"The ghosts of the men you murdered—because they bid lower than their ideological enemies at the Peer by the river for the goods you now rape from this land—will have their revenge on you, *Sasha*," she replied with steel in her voice, her mouth half-filled with teeth.

Her reward for honesty, mental discipline, and unflinching bravery? More teeth knocked loose, courtesy of the butt of Alexander's vintage revolver.

"What did you do that for, Sasha?!" Stefan growled, bending to lift from the muddy ground the woman who had once been his beloved teacher—and, during his most lucid time on mild doses of Scientifica, his most trusted mentor as Philosopher King of our fledgling country.

"She called me *Sasha*," Alexander said glibly. "And if you call me by that pet name you gave me as a harmless boy you wanted to turn into yourself..." He pressed the cold metal of the revolver barrel into my forehead.

"Whatever you say, *Alexander*," my former ward, friend, master—and now fellow prisoner—said with a deep, courtly bow.

With that, Alexander mounted Natasha and trotted her toward the Presidential Cabin, the one that had once belonged to his father. Father Basili approached, arm-in-arm with his secretary, both reeking of semen, their pockets clinking with coins and overflowing with paper currency from seven different nations. From beneath his Cossack, the priest pulled out a shovel and handed it to Stefan.

"Your turn to dig your way out of the mess you made—which, thank God, now benefits *us*," he said smugly, crossing himself. He gestured toward a feces-covered corral, filled with horses branded by the Red, White, Black, and Expeditionary Forces. A "For Sale" sign hung on the fence. Their riders, of course, had all mysteriously 'disappeared.'

"I will pray for you, of course," Basili said, sanctimoniously. "Intercede to the Lord on your behalf as you do your penance—as a shit-shoveler, rather than a shit-distributor."

"For a fee, of course," Stefan replied, staring hard at the corrupt priest he had once exposed to his flock and exiled from Ivankovia after his first dose of Scientifica.

"Of course," Basili answered, either oblivious to Stefan's disgust or simply indifferent. It was as though he were afflicted by some soul-sickening disease that forced the mind to believe bad was good, greed was virtue, and honesty the lowest form of communication. Perhaps it was the Scientifica speaking. Or perhaps not.

As for me, I followed Stefan toward the corral, only to make a quick getaway into the woods. A guard—whom I didn't recognize—was already preparing to stick a price tag on my ear. I kicked him in the knee mid-motion, sending his fat ass tumbling into a heap of manure. Stefan smirked, satisfied. A moment later, the price tag destined for my forehead was slapped onto his.

# CHAPTER 27

There are many differences between humans—presumably the most advanced species on land—and the rest of the mammals. The opposable thumb, for instance, which primates and humans use to grasp objects from the ground—or steal them from others. Skin that clings tightly to the body beneath it, which humans share with pigs. And then, there are the eyes.

In humans, half the information from the right eye travels to the left brain, and vice versa. But there is something we so-called "lower" mammals possess that humans do not: the *tapetum lucidum*—a layer behind the eyes that allows us to be seen at night. Humans lack it. And so, in the dark, our eyes terrify them. All they see is a pair of glowing orbs, with no clue what kind of beast is watching them from the shadows.

I used that to my advantage, scaring off Iankovians and their "invited" guests whenever I spied on them after sunset. As long as I moved like a rabid moose or a man-eating cougar, no one dared pursue me. That gave me time to observe—to see how the first became last, and the last became first. More importantly, it helped me locate the stash of *Scientifica*. Perhaps an extra dose would give Stefan the edge over "Alexander." Or perhaps it would turn him into something far worse. But one thing was certain: if Alexander gave any more of the intelligence-enhancing serum to his minions, Iankovia's days as an independent country were numbered. And if he was selling it to the highest bidder, the rich would become richer, the powerful even more tyrannical, and the haves would strip the have-nots of what little remained—until this continent, this planet, became uninhabitable for any creature that dared to care or share.

Despite my naturally auburn coat, keen hearing, an unseasonably warm month (with more windows left open), and the gracious alignment of the astronomical gods—clouds shrouding the moon and a few nights with no moon at all—I still couldn't locate the stash of *Scientifica*, nor identify who was distributing it. Even Alexander never spoke of it—not to others, not to himself—not even in his half-conscious mumblings when rattling off policy in the solitude of his new "royal" abode. And as for talking in his sleep or dreaming aloud? My ears caught only his snoring. He now slept in his father's private cabin, behind the house he'd grown up in. What was once a modest Cossack shelter had been transformed into a cottage adorned with the ornaments and furnishings of Czarist nobility.

By day, I hid in the woods, peeking through thick brush to see how Stefan endured life at the bottom of the totem pole. He had been relegated to the role of a servant—chronically dirty, foul-smelling, blistered, aching, and exhausted. He was mocked, overworked, spat on. And worst of all, he was smarter—painfully so—than any of his new masters. That awareness made the abuse more unbearable. The agony was sharpened by his refusal to accept the still-repeated motto: *God rewards you in Heaven according to how much you suffer on Earth.* Something that we horses—some of us, at least—understood far too well.

And speaking of horses... I witnessed more than a few fine saddle horses sent to the slaughterhouse to serve as meat for the visiting dignitaries. Others were sold to the highest bidder—often officers from foreign armies—men who were both cruel and ignorant of what these horses could do, and what would break them. My heart ached for each of them. But none so much as for Natasha.

Natasha was the Emperor's favorite—a proud white mare. He rode her with a cruel hand: a tight rein forcing her neck into her fly-bitten chest, spurs tearing holes into her flanks, and a silver-coated saddle five times heavier than necessary. Each day, more saddlebags and satchels were piled onto her back. Yet out of habit—or fear of the slaughterhouse—she obeyed. She never let anyone see that she was lame in her right front and left hind legs. Because if Alexander noticed, he'd replace her. Another white horse would be chosen to showcase his so-called acrobatic Cossack skills. A title no true Cossack would ever respect.

There were horses worse off than Natasha, but she had become *family* to me. My heart chose her, and my selective compassion clung to her pain. I'll never forget the "dance" Alexander made her perform on an especially bitter day, for an entourage of high-rolling civilian bidders—unarmed, as far as I could tell—representing the Red, White, Black, and Expeditionary Force Armies, their lapel flags a clear giveaway.

The performance left her drenched in sweat, her chest dripping to the earth, blood oozing from her mouth. And yet, he grinned.

"Welcome, gentlemen, to my country," he declared proudly, his soldiers discreetly forming a circle around the buyers. "Before the bidding begins—for our oil, wheat, horses, valuable miners, and the special medicinals that make us *invincible*—a song from my beloved mother, and a dance from my talented sister."

Svetlana sashayed out of the tavern in a traditional Cossack dress that flowed gracefully to her ankles. Her song, performed in a dialect of Cossack Ukrainian, was a feast for the ears—though none of the buyers understood it, nor cared to. Still, it resonated with the uniformed officers and black-suited businessmen alike.

Tanya followed, wearing considerably less. She danced her way into the open, captivating the buyers' attention. As she drew closer to them, she stroked each of their cheeks with a smile that whispered, *"I like you the best,"* to every man in the room.

While the buyers were developing third legs between the ones they were born with, Alexander led Natasha to the corral. After leaping off the saddle with exaggerated flair, he gripped her reins just as she was about to enter the pen to the right—the one reserved for high-priced riding horses, with invisible price tags glued to their foreheads and ears.

"No, bitch," he grunted at the horse—careful to stay out of earshot of the buyers. "You go into *that* pen." He yanked her toward the left, the pen marked *For Meat Sale: Old, Diseased, or Infirmed.*

He opened the gate and pulled her inside. The mostly healthy horses behind him backed away, hesitant to seize the fleeting chance to escape. After forcing Natasha into the corral, Alexander turned to lock the gate. But before he could, he felt a hard object from a powerful place crash into his left leg.

I adjusted my still sound right leg to deliver another reminder of his mortality—this time, right into his ass—sending him tumbling into a pile of manure. Then I yanked the gate open with my mouth, giving Natasha and the others the chance to bolt.

Laughter erupted from the buyers. I had to look—had to reward myself with the sight. The spectacle of top buyers laughing at the newly minted mob boss of Iankovia was too tempting to resist. Oh, how glorious it was to feast on the expression on Alexander the Great's face as he was demoted to *Sasha the Slob,* right in front of the buyers and his fellow citizens. I whinnied with satisfaction, tossing my head toward the buyers as if to say, *Bid too low and you won't be buying stew—you'll be in it.*

"A show, put on for your amusement, gentlemen," Tanya interjected smoothly, resuming her dance. "Right,

Svetlana?" she added, addressing her mother like a subordinate.

"Yes, indeed, a show," Svetlana echoed, though her eyes betrayed fear—worrying what her son might do to her for not speaking before her daughter. "Arranged by all of us, who—"

"—will be providing you with the finest carnal entertainment upstairs in the tavern," Alexander interrupted, slipping back into his Sasha persona. "Offered by the most enchanting women east of the Caucasus, before the bidding begins. A customary service." He gestured toward his mother. "Our best provider, of course, is Svetlana."

Svetlana said nothing. For reasons I still don't fully understand, she had been forced into her new role as a sperm recipient. Perhaps she feared the two worst outcomes of being an employee rather than the operator of a brothel: the wrath of God if the abortionist Sasha had hired did her job well... or the gaze of a child, ten years from now, silently asking, *Who is my father?*

Which of the buyers believed it was all part of the show, and which saw the horse escape for what it truly was—I couldn't say. But I do remember one thing with painful clarity: the smallest of the gentlemen, his accent disturbingly similar to the Austrian officer who once conscripted me into the cavalry during the last war. A war that nearly destroyed me, where I was forced to obey commands like a beast of burden—thrown at tanks and machine guns as the lead horse in every suicidal charge.

"I would like to buy that horse," he said, pointing directly at me. "I bid five hundred American dollars."

"Sold!" Alexander declared, no doubt recognizing the value of five hundred American dollars. Unlike the rapidly devaluing Deutschemarks, rubles, or French francs, U.S. currency would hold its worth—at least for another fortnight.

"He's yours," Alexander added.

"If you can catch him," the Red Army representative muttered with a smirk, just as I bolted out of town—driven as much by fear of that Germanic buyer as by concern for Iankovia's fate. I had to find Stefan. Fortunately, he was across the river, shoveling manure for one of Sasha's lesser cronies.

"One hundred dollars to anyone who can catch that performance horse!" the German-accented gentleman bellowed, raising another crisp C-note high for the general public to see.

What followed was a massive manhunt for me—citizens mounted on horseback, seated in cars, or astride motorcycles, all eager to earn a quick hundred dollars. Fortunately, I managed to evade them. The thick brush hindered many of the pursuit horses, and the mud slowed down every vehicle and cart—each one burdened by the so-called miracle of human ingenuity: the wheel.

As for the entourage of money-hungry, soul-dead—but still clever—pursuers trailing behind us, the main body of the "to-be-turned-into-hamburger" herd lingered at the edge of the chase, grazing on patches of luscious grass. It was likely the first decent grass they'd tasted in weeks. After being branded as meat, they were worth more dead than alive—to the millions of civilians and soldiers scattered across the rest of Russia at the time.

Eventually, I caught up with Natasha. She was out of breath but not out of purpose. I could feel her saying to me: *Andrei would never put me through all of this. He has to be here somewhere.*

*"So,"* I replied, in the only language she and I truly shared—telepathy. *"We should try to find Andrei. If he's still alive."*

I knew I was lying again. Offering her hope I didn't truly believe in. Still, I pressed on. *"I think I know where we can find someone who can help us,"* I added, motioning toward a small hamlet across the river—an emerging town with more buildings than farms now.

Yes, I was really trying to find and rescue Stefan. As for Andrei... Natasha's only real chance of reuniting with her long-lost master and friend was to throw herself off a cliff and hope for a reincarnation miracle—returning in the right body, in the right time, in the right world.

But you see, there was a truth the horse buyers from every army—especially those from non-Cossack regions—didn't know, or refused to understand:

A Cossack horse will do *anything* its master asks.

Even charge into cannon fire.

That's what I was counting on.

And praying for.

# CHAPTER 28

One thing I observed during the day, from various hiding places within Iankovia, was that Stefan took his first-class medical kit with him to every lowliest, non-medical job he was assigned—because he was the wisest man in the country. It was a fate he shared with Mrs. Lubinska, who was, perhaps, even wiser.

I didn't always see what he did at each stop, but every evening, he returned from those shit jobs with fewer medical supplies than he left with. And yet, each morning, he emerged from the shack behind the former hospital—now a slaughterhouse and tannery—with a refilled pack on his shoulders. How many people or animals he treated during his internal exile, I didn't know. What kind of gratitude they gave him, I could only guess—but likely the same kind offered in the pre-scientifica days of the Great War, when being a great doctor was just expected. And being gifted in reassembling flesh torn by trauma or disease meant you had failed at being a manipulator of men. Because the Good Lord had neglected to give you that more "useful" ability.

I watched him one evening from across the river, just before sundown. He was walking home from cleaning Kornikov's pig pens, horse stalls, newly installed indoor toilets, and overflowing septic tanks. The small rowboat he'd left on the riverbank that morning still lay there—now riddled with shotgun holes along the bottom, which he only discovered when he tried to cast off and return "home."

I whinnied to him. He waved back.

Then I walked—then swam—across the river to meet him, cutting through a layer of oil spilled from a transport boat. After shaking the water from my back, and failing to rid myself of the oil clinging underneath, I turned, lay down in the water, and let Doctor Stefan step over me with his tired feet.

He fashioned a rope into a bridle, rigged it as a hackamore, then secured the medical kit to his back.

"Thank you," he whispered, stroking my neck with the same affection and respect he used to show when I was just the platoon clown.

You're very welcome, I snorted back.

We made our way across the shallows by foot, then paddled toward Natasha, who greeted us from the far bank with a whinny that said, *Hey—I'm here. Don't leave me like this.*

Once we reached the other side—what had once, two weeks ago, been a clean stream of flowing water—Stefan slid off my bare back and wiped the film of oil from my body. He removed the saddle and other burdens Sasha had strapped to Natasha, placing the essential gear onto me instead. Then he removed the bit from her mouth, noting the blood seeping from her gums, and flung it into the water.

As the sun retired behind a smog-drenched horizon, the moon rose, illuminating the ground in a silver wash. We could see every pebble around us. And worse—be seen by anyone searching for us. Maybe bounty hunters, better armed than the three of us, lurking in the woods.

Sensing this, Stefan drew a traditional Cossack battleaxe from beneath his belt. Its edge had been dulled from chopping endless stacks of firewood—wood he would never get to warm himself by. He tracked the movement of a single bounty hunter using only his ears. Guided by rustling brush, Stefan darted ahead of the figure, back turned, and set a snare to trap the intruder's feet.

That's when he saw what I had already smelled— traces of blood and rotting flesh on the branches. It gave me concern. It sent Natasha into a quiet panic.

"A dying animal," Stefan whispered to us. "One we'll have to put out of its misery—and ours."

He crouched behind a fallen tree, axe raised, eyes locked on the shadows.

Then it fell. The intruder collapsed onto the riverbank—flesh raw, entrails hanging from its belly, fur covered in cloth. The face—drenched in blood and dirt—was unrecognizable. A dying, half-scalped man? A woman?

"Hide me... help me," the creature wheezed with a very human death rattle. The voice cleared the field of birds and mice. It pointed weakly to higher ground on the riverbank.

"Whoever you are, I'll do my best to help you," Stefan said, fully aware of the danger. If Alexander's patrols—those soldier-citizens—found this broken body, it would cost Stefan everything.

He tore through his medical kit, grabbing a loaded vial of opium. Then another three, after assessing the full extent of the damage—beyond even what his old-world talents, amplified by scientifica, could now repair.

"No! Not yet," the patient gasped.

That voice—I recognized it instantly.

Natasha did too. She snorted with relief and nuzzled his face.

With all the strength left in his skinned-alive arm, he stroked her neck.

"Andrei?" Stefan asked—afraid of the answer.

"I had to come back... to warn you about..." The rest dissolved into garbled speech, blood trickling from his lips.

"Sasha—who…" Stefan began, but stopped himself. There was no point in telling Andrei that he might be too late.

"—is someone else now… because he got into…" Andrei forced through a mouth nearly empty of teeth.

"Something he shouldn't have?" Stefan asked gently.

"Yeah… Something I suspected but never…" More blood. This time, frothy—chunks of lung tissue mixed in.

"I know," Stefan said. "Or… I suspected. Now that he—"

"Mrs. Lubinska," Andrei interrupted. "The teacher you admired. The one I took for granted. She always said God never gives a problem without…"

"…a solution," Stefan finished.

"But since God is…"

"…on a long supper break," Stefan offered, almost smiling.

"It's Nature now," Andrei muttered, face ghost-white beneath the caked blood. "Nature never gives you a problem without a solution."

"She also said…" Andrei struggled to point to a folded paper in his pocket.

"'Beware of gardens of toxic happiness and effortless success,'" Stefan read aloud.

"I rode through it… by accident. The place she warned us never to go. But now…"

He gestured toward his breast pocket.

"…it's where we have to go?" Stefan guessed, catching the scent of leaves wafting out. "This herb… is…"

"…the antidote. Maybe. For whatever it is Sasha got into—and meant to give me?"

"Yes. You were on the list," Stefan admitted. "A privileged list that I…"

He faltered, hating himself for delaying the gift of scientifica to those who truly deserved it.

"Andrei, I'm sorry that I…"

Andrei—older, usually less morally evolved—grabbed his brother's arm.

"North by northwest," he whispered, pointing. "Follow the trail of happy wolves who lost their ambition to hunt… to where their prey lies dead but smiling… maybe from eating too much of that," he said, nodding toward the leaves. "Maybe God—or Nature—left it as the solution to…"

Andrei, breath heavy with the loco leaves, broke into a final, fragile smile.

Then he exhaled one last time.

It made sense to me, just as it did to Stefan.

We knew what had to be done.

But *how* to do it?

And *where* was the storage place for scientifica? How could we neutralize it with what Mrs. Lubinska had called *toxic happy weed*?

Could we sneak it into the bodies of those who were poisoning our town, our country—and our vision?

But first, we had to reach the happy valley.

And do it undetected by the posse that was now surely closing in.

# CHAPTER 29

I remember, from the time I inhabited a body expected to know how to read, that people judge a book by its cover. Racists—which, in some way or another, we all are—judge others by the color of their skin. They decide what to say based on how thick the skin of the person being spoken to appears. And above that skin is hair. Its pattern, color, and quantity are part of the picture we use to define who we are—or to hide behind, so others can't see who and what we truly are.

I heard Stefan tell more than one curious child, suspicious officer, or intrigued woman that if he ever shaved off the mustache he'd grown at sixteen, there would be puddles of blood on the floor. As for the closely cropped hair around his thick Cossack warlock braid, he claimed that letting the rest of his hair grow into a long mane would block the signals from Heaven trying to reach his brain.

So it surprised me to see my master become a "mastress" just to find out where Sasha had stored the Scientifica powder—and to spike it with cannabis leaves, also known as "toxic happy weeds." The plan was to delay the evil schemes envisioned by the new users of Scientifica. Weed, after all, has a way of making people put things off.

To accomplish both goals, Stefan had to use something other than balls. I never learned the female equivalent of that term, but with some hair from my tail glued inside a hat, a bit of blood from his fingers dabbed on his lips, and the removal of his mustache, Stefan passed easily as a cleaning woman—forty going on eighty.

As for me, in order not to be recognized as Enemy Number One in the New Iankovian Republic, Stefan rubbed my coat with black coal and brown sand, turning me into a common workhorse—free to roam our not-so-fair community without being shot or kidnapped. It worked as long as I shuffled my feet and kept my head low enough to watch the upturned-chinned elite without drawing their attention. The same disguise worked for "Stefanie."

A horse's eyes can't see clearly beyond fifty feet, but our noses make up for that. We can sniff out danger in the woods before any two-legged human can—bears, wolves, or, said quietly to you, kind reader, drunk hunters who can't tell the difference between a horse, elk, or deer. That nose of mine could also detect where the Scientifica was stored.

It was in the one place few Iankovians dared venture under Alexander's rule. A place where both believers and skeptics lost their grip on reason. A place no one would think to look.

The back room of the church.

The so-called "holy place" where Father Basili either spoke with God—or sweet-talked vulnerable boys, girls, and nuns. The smell drew me in. The gossip Stefan—excuse me, "Stefanie"—heard while cleaning the homes of the new Iankovian elite confirmed it.

The time to act came on a Sunday afternoon. Father Basili was blessing a new series of oil wells—yet another violation of Mother Nature's sacred ground. Everyone who was anyone, or who didn't want to remain a nobody, was required to attend.

"So," Stefan, as Stefanie, said in a voice two octaves higher than his usual baritone while easily unlocking the door to the church's back room, "maybe Sasha is offering something he values even more than prayer. Maybe he's putting it in the bread Father Basili hands out at communion."

He stepped inside the private chamber—a room supposedly reserved for angels, a space where any commoner who dared enter would surely lose their eyes, just like the priest chambers in the Acropolis maintained by ancient pagan Greeks before they became "Christianized."

"How do Sasha and Basili decide who's worthy of receiving the 'blessings' of advanced intelligence, courtesy of Scientifica?" Stefan asked aloud.

The answer came to me instantly. I trotted over to the side window and gave Stefan a soft nicker, directing his attention toward the conversations echoing from the church's new confessional booths—what Basili called the "interrogation rooms."

"Of course," Stefan said, spotting the recently constructed confessionals. A very *Catholic* addition to his allegedly Eastern Orthodox church. They encouraged believers to confess sins and be forgiven… and allowed non-believers to spill their secrets without consequence.

Only here, unlike in true churches, and unlike Oksana—the gypsy whore who could coax secrets from men and women alike under dim lights—it wasn't the most repentant who were rewarded. It was the cleverest. The most devious. Those smart enough to remain loyal to Pope Alexander were promoted into the "intelligentsia" class with Scientifica.

"I wonder who's listening on the other side of these booths," Stefan muttered, opening the clergyman's door to investigate. But the intel gatherers had left no trace. Stefan cursed with such furious expletives that he might've earned himself a one-way ticket to hell. And he might've gotten there fast—had I not smelled, and then heard, Basili approaching with four heavily armed guards in Alexander's new military uniform. Their Master walked with them.

I gave Stefan a sharp warning nicker.

He immediately dropped to his knees, bowed his head, crossed himself, and began scrubbing the floor with a rag tucked into the belt of his dress.

Basili sent the guards into the listening chambers. Sasha entered the back room—ironically, the very space where he'd once served as an altar boy just five years earlier. He opened the lock on the most worn chest in the room, whispering the numbers as he dialed them: six to the right, six to the left, and six to the left again. I remembered hearing him mumble the same code once, when he thought neither God, man, nor horse was listening. I tapped out the combination to Stefan with alternating hooves.

"What I suspected already," Stefan whispered, crossing himself again.

Sasha counted the bags of powdered Scientifica. He scooped a fist-sized portion into a bowl of holy water, then swallowed it with greedy satisfaction. Next, he opened a gold-plated Bible and examined a list inside, crossing off some names, adding others. He removed three smaller bags from the chest, tucked them into his coat, and re-locked it.

Before leaving, he paused in the sanctuary to study a carved wooden image of Christ on the cross—one that Stefan had sculpted from a tree he claimed had more of the Holy Spirit than any other in the forest.

"Hmph," Sasha said to the Savior's likeness—or perhaps to the man who carved it. "You were a sucker." He smirked. "Still are."

He helped himself to a few more coins from the poor box, then strode out of the church with his entourage— passing by the kneeling cleaning woman without so much as a glance.

"Now, it's our turn," Stefan whispered once the coast was clear.

He retrieved three large bags of locoweed powder hidden beneath his dress and slipped into the sacred chamber. He opened the chest and carefully added the drug into the Scientifica bags in measured proportion. Every detail mattered. After he finished, he looked up at the carving of Jesus—the one he himself had shaped—and said softly:

"Yes, I was a sucker. And maybe you were too. But, as you found out way too late... Heaven watches, and Earth works."

# CHAPTER 30

Stefan and I lingered in the woods, hiding in caves by day and roaming under cover of night. I was—between owners anyway—like a wild horse, used to sniffing out forageable grass. Stefan, thanks to his late grandfather, was a skilled hunter, fisherman, and gatherer of edible herbs. As for my share of nature's bounty, the lush grasslands of the Steppes in and around Iankovia had long since been converted into oil fields, mineral mines, or agricultural zones—each one guarded, day and night, with relentless vigilance.

Stefan couldn't snare a rabbit, catch a fish, or bring down even the slowest, most decrepit elk—not because of his lack of skill, but because there were simply none to be found. Or perhaps the animals had grown wise, developing an intelligence that helped them avoid us.

By the fifth day of waiting just outside Iankovia—hoping to observe what effect Sasha's cannabis-laced scientifica would have on its consumers—our stomachs were growling loudly enough to scare off any potential prey.

"Time to get what we need from the granary and slaughterhouses," Stefan said as the sun climbed above a soot-stained horizon.

I nickered in agreement—not a bad idea. The mere mention of the word grain stirred memories of better-fed days, despite the risk of overeating and becoming foundered.

From our high vantage point overlooking the capital, we saw that the once-overfilled granary was now nearly empty. The meat hooks in the slaughterhouse hung bare. General store shelves, once overflowing, were reduced to scattered remnants. Bakeries boasted crumbs as the day's special.

Well-fed elites, handpicked by Sasha and his "guests," waddled from shop to shop, their bellies distended, growing more intoxicated with every step. They stumbled through their supervisory duties like drunken zombies—utterly content, yet devoid of urgency or purpose. Among them, dancing in delusional euphoria, were Stefan's wife and daughter—blissfully unaware of their condition, as though they were performers on a stage, dancing to a song only they could hear.

Father Basili—the notoriously homophobic priest— paraded about in his secretary's dress and petticoats, singing praises to Jesus as his bridegroom, proudly claiming himself as the bride. Meanwhile, his secretary wore the "good Father's" robes and roamed the streets blessing rats, mice, and insects in a language I couldn't recognize.

And Sasha's lieutenants? Instead of scheming together to turn a profit for themselves and their unseen masters, they bumped into one another like billiard balls on a drunken table. After a few too many "excuse me, Comrade Asshole" encounters, they collapsed where they stood—sinking into sleep, heavy and stupefied.

"The more they eat the happy-weed-spiked scientifica Sasha's been feeding them, the less energy they have," Stefan observed. "Maybe we should've laced the grain and meat too—to lull the well-fed bastards into overstuffed slumber. Or into being corpses. But…"

His long silence unsettled me. I followed his gaze toward the oil rigs, pumping black gold into the air, choking the sky with soot. The mines were running at record speeds, tearing minerals from the ground while decimating the life that once thrived above it.

At the docks, a new foreman was collecting satchels of cash from no fewer than three captains of overloaded, unmarked ships. After a quick military-style salute and handshake, the foreman turned—and we saw the smirking face of none other than Sasha.

After counting the money, the Emperor—disguised in rags—looked straight up at us, pointing deliberately toward the village square.

There, women I didn't recognize were screaming at the laundry ladies, furious that bloodstains remained on uniforms once worn by buyers who hadn't bid high enough for the goods they sought. Nearby, very sober men—likely from the lower rungs of society, squeezed under both Stefan's old rule and Sasha's new greed—collapsed in the dust, stripped of strength and hope. And from the sidelines, Mrs. Lubinska spotted us, offering only a shrug, as if to say, I don't know why either.

"So, Sasha's making another list," Stefan muttered, his voice tight. "Choosing who deserves scientifica—by his 'Imperial Code'—to keep his empire afloat. Likely a batch that wasn't tainted with locoweed. Or maybe he's found another supply that's…"

As if reading his father's thoughts, Sasha pointed at Stefan and beckoned him down the hill—just as the ship at the dock hoisted the Red Army flag.

"I thought you'd agree," Sasha shouted up to us, wiggling his fingers ever so slightly in invitation.

It wasn't a request. Three well-armed soldiers of the New Iankovian Republic stepped behind us, rifles trained on our backs.

"Everyone gives according to their abilities, and takes according to their needs," Sasha called out—quoting Marx and Engels in a voice eerily similar to his father's. "A spiritual mandate you once said Jesus would agree with. To the Whites, I gave—after discovering what you'd slipped into it—a generous portion of scientifica... the altered kind."

"And the Anarchists and Expeditionary Forces?" Stefan asked as the soldiers escorted him down. "Did you toast them with vodka and offer them a night of passion with the women you turned into whores—only to have them die in their beds, betrayed by a knife to the heart?"

"They always were whores," Sasha said with a smirking arrogance. "And it was a bullet to the head. Quicker. Cleaner. Lets us sell the rest of the body for meat—and there's less mess to mop up off the floors. The bullets were…"

"Fired by your sister and mother?" Stefan dared to ask, now standing within a yard of the still-reigning Emperor.

"Do you really want me to answer that question?" Sasha asked, his voice sharp but calm, speaking to the man who had once been his beloved father.

"Yes," Stefan replied, summoning what little courage he still possessed beneath the suffocating weight of fear in his gut.

"Which is why I… won't answer it," the Emperor replied coolly, his smirk deepening. "But I'm sure you have other questions. Questions I'll gladly answer before you can stammer them from those quivering lips of yours," Sasha continued, pacing around us like a general surveying a battlefield—one between heart and brain, both of which he claimed dominion over. He was reading his father's mind... and mine.

"How did I figure out what *scientifica* really does?" he began. "Andrei noticed it first—how, whenever you went off on your solitary rides with this 'assistant' of yours," he said, pointing to me and striking my neck with a sharp lash from his crop. "You'd come back claiming to hear God's voice more clearly... and yet, you returned more distant each time. More removed. That made us curious. So I followed you to the fields where the *scientifica* grew. And as for your next question—how I got into the safe where you kept it, without getting burned or succumbing to the ricin you rigged it with... the box you labeled *Private, Please*..."

He paused for effect.

"I was one of the creatures you never noticed in the woods, watching you outside your private cabin. I saw the combination you entered on the lock. I saw you use gloves."

"And where is the rest of the *scientifica*?" Stefan pressed, this time refusing to accept a vague answer, fully prepared to meet his Maker for daring to demand a real one.

Sasha bared his teeth in a half-laugh, then paused. For a brief second, something flickered in his eyes— contemplation, maybe. Of his own mortality. Then he met his father's gaze—cold, hollow, unflinching.

"At the time of dying," he said flatly. "Yours or mine."

He gave a nod to his second-in-command, who stepped forward carrying a small suitcase. The man—a lieutenant twice as muscular as Sasha and, judging by the vacant glaze in his drug-clouded eyes, only half as intelligent—opened the case with theatrical flair. Inside were two authentic 19th-century Cossack swords.

"A duel," Sasha said, gesturing first to Stefan, then to the men flanking him, "between intelligence linked to the heart—"

"—and intelligence linked to... practicality?" Stefan interjected, though it was clear he had wanted to say *evil*. But he was wise enough not to speak that word aloud in front of the demon masquerading as his son. Not yet.

Yes, I said demon. Satan, if he's real, is the left turn at the fork that dares us to choose the right. Or perhaps he's just a figment of our imagination—something we invented to keep believing that life is a battle between good and evil, when really it might be a search for Truth and Spirit. The former is absolute. The latter... beyond human grasp.

But those were questions for later—if there *was* a later. For now, it was a game. A deadly one. A game between father and son, instigated by the latter but—painfully, in ways Stefan could no longer deny—created by the former.

And it wasn't just father against son. It was Natasha... against me.

Natasha, who had been given a clean, potent dose of *scientifica*, free of locoweed.

"Bring it on," she sneered at me, once a gentle mare, now transformed into a snarling beast. She stepped proudly to Sasha's side, crunching a carrot fed to her from his hand. A strange odor wafted from her mouth—something I didn't recognize.

# CHAPTER 31

There were many things that concerned me about a duel to the death between Stefan and his son. Chief among them was the unsettling fact that, despite Stefan's reverence for his Cossack ancestors, he had never killed a man—or even ordered a death. Conversations I'd overheard from his now-slain Great War comrades confirmed that the most harm Stefan had ever inflicted in that bloody conflict was shooting an enemy in the fleshy part of the leg—so the man could be sent home rather than killed.

His son, Sasha, however, had no such reservations. He had not only permitted but likely participated in the killing of "buyers" who visited Ivanovia and dared to underbid for the goods they sought—especially after his intelligence had been unnaturally enhanced by Scientifica. And perhaps he'd been involved in such atrocities even before Stefan's return and transformation by the plant—whether enchanted or cursed—that changed everything.

Why Sasha, now King Alexander, agreed to a duel with the Philosopher King he had deposed, I couldn't say. Perhaps it was something he needed to prove—to his father, or to himself. Post-Scientifica, Stefan still reminded his son that *"it is a poor student who doesn't surpass his teacher."* Though Stefan's meaning was clear: he was referring to Sasha's God-given healing gifts—not his capacity to take life. To be a servant of humanity, not a conqueror of it.

But, more urgently, to you—dear and patient reader—who has endured my ramblings or perhaps skipped ahead in hope of a climactic end: you are likely expecting a dramatic duel between father and son. One in which Stefan suffers an invisible wound, inflicted by Sasha, to fix the outcome. And, well—you're partly right.

As a self-taught physician and healer, Stefan should have known: if 10 units of an herb bring healing, 20 does not bring double the benefit. Scientifica may have sharpened his mind—quicker, deeper, wiser—but the muscles below his neck suffered almost immediately. After the very first dose, which I administered, Stefan's once-powerful body deteriorated. His legs shriveled into fragile limbs that could barely grip a saddleless horse. His arms, once capable of lifting a man, now struggled to carry a saddle ten feet. He panted heavily if he dared to run or climb even the smallest hill without stopping every ten paces. His once-thick warlock-brown hair thinned to a pale white mane, on the verge of falling out completely.

Some of the physical decline was due to his increasing reliance on his fellow citizens—those he loved more than they loved themselves—to do the hard labor he could no longer manage. Only two years earlier, he had been stronger than any of them.

But none of that stopped Sasha. He allowed his guards to beat Stefan—savagely, repeatedly—in a hidden clearing deep in the woods, far from any human or animal witness. Then, with cruel artistry, he dressed his barely conscious father in a finely tailored 18th-century Cossack uniform. The garb was cut in a way that exaggerated the remnants of his frame, making him appear Herculean in shoulder and limb. Sasha himself wore a custom-designed military uniform—a grotesque amalgam of the finest styles worn by generals of Germany, America, France, and Britain, each nation still clinging to the illusion that the *next* war would end all wars.

And then, he made his announcement: a duel between "old and new," between the "noble and the comfortable." The people of Iankovia, he declared, would decide which century they chose to live in.

The duel's setting was the heart of town—once a sacred gathering place where the elected Hetman summoned the people or was deposed by them. Along the rope fence stood spectators: some rich in comfort, others rich in soul—none, it seemed, rich in both. And at the center stage stood none other than Father Basili, hands raised, giving the event his blessing. He declared that the outcome would be decided by God.

"The loser," he intoned, "will be sent to his just reward."

"Heaven," he said, turning toward Sasha.

"Or hell," he added, glaring—first at Stefan, then, unsettlingly, at me.

My eyes found Natasha—her belly pressed tightly between Sasha's gleaming boots and sharpened spurs. I tried to tell her, in the only way I knew how, that it could be *us* who determined the outcome of this match—not the men towering above us, nor the Deity above them, whose attributes and Will, though more imagined than real, suddenly felt undeniably present. A divine script seemed to unfold, not just for man but for beast.

"Heaven watches, earth works," I snorted to her.

"It's you who'll be horsemeat by the end of this day, not me," she seemed to nicker back. Her eyes, glazed and wild, shone with a madness I could only describe—though it chills me to say—as demonic.

"On the count of three, draw sabres!" Father Basili roared, like a brawling referee presiding over two drunken Cossacks fighting for a woman who'd wandered into the wrong bar after too much vodka.

On the count of three, Sasha raised his blade— gleaming, deadly, freshly sharpened. It blinded me in the sunlight. I heard the reluctant thud of Stefan's dull, edgeless sword dragging from its sheath.

"Into your black, demonically possessed heart!" Sasha bellowed, weapon poised. "I *must* do this to save everyone here from the evil you brought upon us!" His voice thundered with righteous fury. "Justice—swift and clean—to end your misery... and *ours*."

"Slapped onto your backside—for a much-needed spanking," Stefan declared with a smile, referring to his 'butterknife.' "Which will hurt me more than you, son," he confessed with utmost sincerity. "A gift I never gave you—out of ignorance and cowardice."

The crowd offered no audible reaction to either the pledge or the reasoning behind it. Perhaps it was the presence of soldiers in uniforms matching Sasha's, looming behind them. Or maybe it was something in the air—a strange scent, medicinal and sharp, rising from smoky smudges behind the spectators. It resembled the incense Basili and the other priests burned in church to keep the congregation subdued and aware of their sins... but with something else added. Something unfamiliar.

Father and son locked eyes, engaged in a silent exchange about the past, the present, and the futures that might still be written. I didn't try to interpret it—perhaps out of respect for what Sasha might have been, and for what Stefan had finally become. Or perhaps because Natasha was glaring at me, ears pointed toward my face, stomping her hooves as if she intended to drive them deeper into me than into the despondent rider on her back.

"And on the count of ten," Basili announced—as ten seconds stretched into an eternity. To display his pitiful knowledge of three languages, he began the countdown in poorly pronounced French, then German, then English, and finally Ukrainian—with a heavy Russian accent.

Sasha charged forward at full speed, spurring Natasha ahead, his saber gleaming, his body rising from the saddle in a poised attack. Thinking with the same mind—as we did in the old days—Stefan and I bolted forward. Then, just before the moment of impact, we veered hard to the left.

Sasha lost balance as Natasha dipped her head. Amidst a stream of expletives damning his horse, Stefan, and even Jesus to hell, he somehow clambered back into the saddle and yanked Natasha to a jarring stop—just one stride from the crowd.

"Coward!" he shouted at Stefan. "Face me!"

"You'll have to catch me first," Stefan called back with a confident smile—somehow summoning strength in his legs and arms that Scientifica and time had stolen. Reading and sharing each other's thoughts, Stefan and I performed an evasive dance that drew Sasha into charging again and again, missing us each time.

Stefan whipped his dull sword with the same flair and energy he had shown when we performed the Cossack dance for the Austrians during the Great War—impressing, intimidating, and entertaining them into believing we were harmless. Half of the spectators rich in comfort nodded with intrigue. All of the rich in soul smiled.

"All right, let's have done with it, then," Stefan said from the far end of the 'arena,' after driving Sasha into well-earned frustration and embarrassment over nearly falling off his horse.

We charged toward him, Stefan ready to knock him from the saddle with the flat edge of his blade. Then, two strides before impact, he twisted his torso—his body parallel to the not-yet-bloodied ground—forcing Sasha to swing the saber down at him.

All of the rich-in-comfort onlookers broke into secretive smiles. All of the rich-in-soul spectators broke into applause.

Sasha—who, even as a boy, had preferred motorized vehicles over fast-moving beasts with legs and souls—continued charging, growing more exhausted with each wild swing. His attacks tore Stefan's clothes and nearly sliced into my flank. It went on like that for what felt like ten minutes. The most magnificent ten minutes of my life.

Until finally, Sasha hurled his saber away and drew his pistol—first aiming it at Stefan, then at me.

Stefan brought me to an abrupt stop.

"All right, if that's how you want it," he said. Then he leapt off me, the impact sending pain shooting through his feet. "This is between us, Sasha—not the animals who only do what we ask, or force, them to do."

He removed the saddle from my back, motioned for the crowd to clear a path, and slapped my flank. "Be well, my friend," he said with a sense of finality.

I trotted a few strides away, then stopped—wanting, needing—to see what would happen next.

Stefan picked up Sasha's saber, handed it back to him, and motioned for his son to dismount Natasha. Pressured by the crowd, both intimidated and encouraged, Sasha complied. He removed his saddle and turned to send Natasha away.

"Go!" he barked.

She didn't move.

"Now!" he shouted.

Still nothing.

"Please," Stefan said gently, stepping toward her. "This is between us—the lower species. Not you." He whispered into her ear.

Natasha paused. Then walked. Then trotted. Then ran—toward me.

What we said to each other after that… well, I'll share it with you later. For now, we ran into the woods together, stopping at a distance to look back at the humans who used to feed us.

I couldn't see what followed clearly. But I know this: Sasha fought bravely. He inflicted no fewer than five wounds on his father—tearing through fabric and flesh. Stefan defended himself, striking Sasha again and again with the blunt edge of his sword—half of those blows landing squarely on his son's maybe-not-so-accidentally arrogant backside. And the other half? Delivered to the space between Sasha's non-listening ears—where the deepest wounds were made.

The fight between Sasha and Stefan dragged on, feeling as if it might last forever—exhausting the polarized crowd, and finally, the father and son themselves. They knelt on the ground across from one another, gripping their sabers in their right hands, their left hands clenched into fists.

Then, for reasons that astounded me, their left hands opened. Slowly, hesitantly, they extended them toward each other. Their fingers met—not in combat, but in something that resembled a handshake. At the same moment, their right hands released their sabers, letting them fall.

A hush fell over the crowd.

It was a magical moment—a rare, trembling moment where old and new, spiritual and material, masochistic nobility and worldly practicality met in quiet agreement. Just in time for me to hear the rattling gasp of death escape from both father and son.

Still able to read lips, I eavesdropped on their final conversation.

Yes, it was the time of dying. And Sasha, true to his word, honored the promise he had once made: to tell his father where the remaining supply of *Scientifica* was hidden.

"He was an artist in his youth," Sasha said through bloody gasps, red froth bubbling at the corners of his mouth. "Too enthusiastic to be appreciated by the critics. Too dedicated to his craft to be accepted by the elite artists who rejected his application to art school. Too honest in the meaning behind his paintings to win favor with gallery owners who wanted 'emotional subtlety' on canvas. And too determined to make a difference in the world to accept his fate as a well-fed housepainter—one who aspired to nothing more than a contented wife and happy children."

He paused, coughing more blood. "Some of his artwork found its way to me—here. Though I don't know how."

"And the housepainter's name?" Stefan asked gently.

"Adolf," Sasha replied. "An Austrian… in Germany now. Trying to… change the world."

"Through being a successful artist, I hope," Stefan murmured. "Too much passion and power makes a man an ineffective politician, king… or leader. As… well… we both know now."

"Yes," said the self-dethroned Emperor of Iankovia, casting his gaze toward the crowd—the people he and his father had betrayed, tricked, and forced into Visions that were never truly theirs. "Yes. Maybe intelligence isn't the *only* thing one needs to be effectively…"

Sasha collapsed into his father's arms.

"...Compassionate?" Stefan whispered, drawing his final breath.

And with that, Mother Nature gave her response to the long conversation between men, power, and fate.

Mighty Ivan—the oil rig that had once produced the kingdom's most treasured black gold—sank violently into the earth, swallowed by the very ground it had poisoned. The quake it caused disabled the surrounding "Little Ivans," then rumbled and roared its way toward the center of town.

Panic overtook the people. They scattered—some fled into the woods, others to the river, still others into the arms of those they loved.

Only one man remained.

"Father, forgive us! Please!" cried Father Basili, falling to his knees and lifting his voice to the sky. He began to recite the Lord's Prayer, trembling.

"Thy will be done... on earth as it is—"

And then the ground split beneath him.

Did Father Basili ascend to Heaven after being swallowed by the trembling earth, or did he first serve a sabbatical in Hell?

It is not my place to know.

But perhaps it *is* my place to pray—for him, and for all the souls of Iankovia.

And to pray that some of the remaining *Scientifica* found its way to England…

Where a recently deposed Secretary of the Navy named Winston was warning his people that the time to stop Fascism wasn't in the future.

It was now.

With reason.

And Passion.

# ABOUT THE AUTHOR

MJ Politis departed the womb in Hoboken, New Jersey, in 1951.

To make good on what everyone who supported, taught and challenged him did, he obtained a Ph.D. in physiology in 1978 which was used to publish 46 research papers in medical journals in reconstructive neurology, toxicology and cancer treatment.

He went on to obtain a veterinary degree to extend medical care to fur bearing souls in a wide variety of clinics and cultural settings across the US and Canada. In order to diagnose and cure numerous maladies of the human soul, he obtained an H.B.A.R.P. degree (human being, aspiring Renaissance person) as author of over 80 novels and novellas, as well as producer/director/writer on 27 comedo-dramatic films, which can be accessed through:

www.longriderpress.net.

He has been owned by horses for the last 40 years, currently residing in Interior British Columbia, Canada as home base, regularly commuting to New York to maintain global perspective.

Reach out to me at:

mjpolitis@yahoo.com

______________________________